"You cannot live li[...]
reaching with one[...]
his cheek.

It was an intimate gesture, and Rose was aware she had trampled over the boundary that was supposed to separate master and servant, but right now she couldn't find it in herself to care. Every time she looked at him, she saw a man suffering, a man crying out for comfort even though he would never admit it. She could give that comfort.

His eyes locked onto hers and she felt a pulse of attraction pass between them. For a long moment neither of them moved and Rose's fingers felt as though they were burning where they made contact with his skin.

"Rose," he said, and he sounded like a man who was drowning.

She stepped closer so their bodies were almost touching as his hand came up and covered hers, pressing it to his cheek.

"You deserve some happiness," she said, her voice barely more than a whisper.

Author Note

Some books take years in planning. First there is the spark of an idea, slowly nurtured as it builds and grows into a fully fleshed story. Other books I find are quite the opposite. *A Housemaid to Redeem Him* was one of the latter. One late spring evening, I was walking through the wildflower meadows between St Ives and Hemingford Grey in my beautiful little corner of Cambridgeshire. It was one of those idyllic days with golden light and a gentle breeze, and I suddenly thought what a wonderful setting for romance. Even before I had decided on the characters or their stories, I knew I wanted to write about two people, battered and bruised by the world, finding peace and being healed in a place most dear to me.

From there everything built quickly, and even before I was home I knew what Rose and Richard would be like, what they had suffered and how they could make one another happy. I am sure the next book will be one that takes longer to plan, but I am always grateful for those stories that seem to rise almost fully formed.

I hope you enjoy *A Housemaid to Redeem Him*, and as you read I am certain you will fall in love with the meadows of Cambridgeshire as I have.

LAURA MARTIN

A Housemaid to
Redeem Him

HARLEQUIN
HISTORICAL

ISBN-13: 978-1-335-59601-7

A Housemaid to Redeem Him

Copyright © 2024 by Laura Martin

Recycling programs
for this product may
not exist in your area.

This is a work of fiction. Names, characters, places and incidents are either the product of the author's imagination or are used fictitiously. Any resemblance to actual persons, living or dead, businesses, companies, events or locales is entirely coincidental.

For questions and comments about the quality of this book, please contact us at CustomerService@Harlequin.com.

TM and ® are trademarks of Harlequin Enterprises ULC.

Harlequin Enterprises ULC
22 Adelaide St. West, 41st Floor
Toronto, Ontario M5H 4E3, Canada
www.Harlequin.com

Printed in U.S.A.

Laura Martin writes historical romances with an adventurous undercurrent. When not writing, she spends her time working as a doctor in Cambridgeshire, where she lives with her husband. In her spare moments, Laura loves to lose herself in a book, and has been known to read from cover to cover in a single day when the story is particularly gripping. She also loves to travel—especially to visit historical sites and far-flung shores.

Books by Laura Martin

Harlequin Historical

Matchmade Marriages

The Ashburton Reunion

Scandalous Australian Bachelors

Visit the Author Profile page at Harlequin.com for more titles.

For Luke, for those sunny evenings in Houghton and all the walks across the meadows.

Chapter One

As his feet hit the smooth cobbles Richard felt a deep sense of familiarity. Eight years he had been away, eight years of travelling, of wandering, always with his eye on the next place he would visit. He had pushed his home far from his mind, aware of the pain he felt when he thought of everything he had left behind, but now it all came rushing back.

These were the streets of his childhood. He had bought sweets from the shop on the corner, walking home with a mouthful of toffee, feeling as though he was king of the world. His eyes skimmed over the tailor's, where he had been fitted for his first dinner jacket, and the draper's, where his mother would spend hours discussing fabrics while he sat in the corner with his toys.

For a moment he allowed the nostalgia to wash over him, then quickly shook it off. A pleasant reminiscence was not the point of this trip. It was not the reason he had travelled across half the globe. When he had received the letter that gently suggested he return home, he had been helping to rebuild after the devastation of the eruption of Mount Tambora in the Dutch East Indies. The letter from his old childhood friend had arrived, battered and water damaged, many months after it had left England, but it had sparked the trip across the oceans that had eventually brought him back here.

Richard turned away from the market square, walking towards the bridge over the River Great Ouse. From the town it was a fifteen-minute stroll across the meadows to his parents' home in Hemingford Grey. He walked slowly, aware that he was delaying the moment he would have to face his parents again.

The letter from his childhood friend had been artfully written, telling Richard a few pieces of trifling news before moving on to the real point. Sebastian had told him of Richard's father's failing health, of the struggles his mother was going through to look after him. It had gently acknowledged the reasons Richard had left, but encouraged him to put the past behind him and return home.

He dreaded what he might find at Meadow View. When he had left his father had been a strong man, quick to laughter and jolly in nature. He hardly ever fell ill and was proud of his robust constitution.

As Richard walked on to the bridge he felt someone brush past him and the almost imperceptible graze of fingers against his torso. He had spent the last eight years in some of the poorest countries of the world, surrounded by the desperate and the criminal. At first he had often fallen foul of the skills of the pickpockets and street thieves, but over the years his instincts had sharpened and now he knew all the tricks he could employ to keep his possessions safe.

With lightning speed he reached out and grabbed the arm of the young woman who had slipped her hand inside his jacket, grasping her wrist firmly so she could not escape.

She cried out in surprise and spun to face him and he found himself looking into rich brown eyes and a pretty heart-shaped face. The young woman was frowning and tried to pull her arm away.

'What are you doing?' she said, her accent marking her out as not from this rural part of Cambridgeshire with its London drawl.

'I felt your hand in my jacket,' he said, holding her eye. 'You were trying to steal from me, young lady.'

'I was doing no such thing,' she said, trying to tug her wrist from his grip. 'Let go of me.'

'As soon as I let go you'll run.'

'Do you blame me? I'm walking along innocently, minding my own business, and then a strange man accosts me and holds me prisoner.'

'I am hardly holding you prisoner,' he said. He calmed the roil of irritation that welled inside him. It was another known tactic of the petty thieves, one they employed if they were caught in their crimes. Loudly they would deny all knowledge of the crime, calling on other passers-by for aid, accusing their victim of assaulting them.

The young woman pulled her wrist sharply and then looked at him pointedly. 'I am not free to walk away, therefore you are holding me prisoner.'

'Give me my coin purse back.'

'I don't have your coin purse.'

'Give it back to me with no further fuss and I will not haul you in front of the authorities.'

'I don't have your coin purse,' she said, an edge to her voice now.

'Let me phrase it a different way. Delay any longer and I will take pleasure in handing you over to the local magistrate and letting him know quite how much money was in my purse. If you are lucky, you'll be transported.'

Fire danced in the young woman's eyes and he saw her square her shoulders and straighten her back.

'Take me to the magistrate. Once we are standing in front of him you can check your pockets and find your coin purse is exactly where you left it. I can even see the tell-tale bulge in your jacket.'

He glanced down and at that moment she lunged in and stamped on his foot so hard he lost his grip on her. She was wearing heavy boots and put her whole weight behind the move. Darting to one side, she placed herself out of his reach, but didn't flee through the streets as he expected her to. Instead, she stood a few feet away, watching him warily.

'Check your pocket,' she said, motioning to his jacket. 'And then I expect a grovelling apology.'

Slowly, keeping his eyes locked on the young woman, he raised his hand and slipped it inside his jacket. He was surprised to find the coin purse there, sitting snugly in the concealed pocket, undisturbed. He frowned. He was sure he had felt the dance of her fingers over his shirt and wasn't often mistaken in matters such as these.

'It is there, is it not?' she said, boldly taking a step towards him.

'It is.'

'Well?'

Richard looked at the petite blonde woman, realising what a disservice he had done her.

'Please accept my profound apologies, Miss…?'

'You don't need my name,' she said sharply. 'Next time, perhaps check if you have been robbed before throwing around accusations.' With a flick of her head she spun and strode off, ignoring him as he called out after her.

Chapter Two

Meadow View was an impressive house built fifty years earlier by a clever architect who had endeavoured to make the most of the spectacular views from the plot of land available. The result was a beautiful sandy-coloured stone house with vistas of the River Great Ouse from two sides and a magnificent garden that ran down to the banks. The downside was each winter everyone residing in Meadow View would nervously watch as the water level rose and the river burst its banks, hoping desperately it would not reach the house.

There was a sweeping drive up to the front of the house, the entrance on a quiet lane at one end of the village. Today the gates stood open, inviting Richard in.

He was aware he was not expected. Many months ago he had sent a letter to his mother, letting her know he was starting the arduous journey home, but there was no guarantee it had ever reached her. Other letters followed from his stops in India and Egypt and finally Italy, but the system was slow and unreliable and even if she had received one of his missives she would not know when exactly he would be back.

It took him a moment to summon the courage to walk back through the gates. Eight years he had been away and, until recently, he had not thought he would ever return home. His exile was self-inflicted, but he had imagined it would be lifelong.

Oak and horse chestnut trees lined the drive, creating a canopy above his head and providing shade for the first part of the walk to St Ives when it was hot weather. Today those trees were heavy with green leaves and all around him were signs that summer was well on its way.

After a few minutes the house came into view and Richard paused. It looked almost the same as when he had last set eyes on it and he felt a bolt of discomfort when he thought of everything he had missed in the years he had been away. He forced himself to move again, focusing on putting one foot in front of the other until he was directly outside the front door.

He knocked and the door was opened after a few seconds to reveal a smartly dressed footman in the familiar hallway. The footman was young, far too young for him to have been employed when Richard was last home, and smiled at him politely, but with no recognition in his eyes.

'Richard Digby,' he said, passing the man his bag. He always travelled light, with just a few essentials packed in a small bag that he could easily carry himself.

'Mr Digby,' the footman said, flustered. 'We were not expecting you yet.'

He should have sent a letter when he disembarked the ship in Southampton, or at least dispatched a fast messenger with a note when he reached London, but if he was honest with himself he had wanted the chance to change his mind, to turn around and head back to where no one knew him or knew of his past actions.

'Are my parents in?'

'Your mother is in the morning room.'

Richard didn't wait for the footman to say any more, striding through the hall with the portraits of his ancestors looking down and into the morning room.

His mother had aged in the eight years since he had last seen her, although she was still immaculately presented. Her hair had streaks of grey and her face a few more wrinkles, but the absolute joy on her face when she saw him took years off her appearance.

'Richard,' she said, standing and embracing him. He pulled her close, enjoying the warmth he had always shared with his mother. 'We were not expecting you yet. I did not know you had landed in England.'

'I am sorry, I should have written, but I wanted to surprise you.'

'This is the best surprise, the very best,' she said and then promptly burst into tears.

Richard held her tight, letting her sob into his shoulder as he tried to suppress the lump in his throat. His guilt was almost overwhelming. In the time he had been away he had, of course, known his family would miss him, grieve his absence, but he had not allowed himself to really think about what that meant.

'I'm sorry,' he murmured, apologising for so many things.

'Look at me,' his mother said with a hint of a smile. 'I'll drive you away again with my crying.'

'No, you won't.'

Lady Digby took a step back and regarded him, letting her eyes flick over his face and body before giving a nod of satisfaction.

'I worried you would be wasting away, living in those exotic places, always chasing the next disaster to throw yourself at.'

He smiled ruefully. 'Chasing the next disaster' wasn't a bad way to describe how he had lived his life the last few years. After leaving England he had lacked purpose, but had the strong urge to do some good in the world. He had spent some time outside New York, helping to rebuild and replant damaged crops after a hurricane had wreaked havoc. Then he had moved on, looking for the next place that needed a strong physique and volunteers to help after storms and earthquakes and, most recently, a devastating volcanic eruption that had led to a terrible famine.

'But you look well, Richard, strong,' she said.

'You look well, too, Mother, although a little tired.'

Lady Digby gave a sigh filled with emotion. 'I am tired.'

'How is Father?'

There was the glint of tears again in his mother's eyes and he felt a gnawing anxiety as she bade him to sit.

'I think Sebastian wrote to you, am I right?'

'He did.'

'He's a good boy. He visits every week when he is back from London and brings a hamper filled with the best produce from his estate.'

Richard suppressed a smile at his mother calling Sebastian Harper a *good boy*. The man was thirty, well over six foot tall, and had been the Earl of Cambridgeshire for the last six years.

'What did he say?'

'That Father was unwell, that his memory was failing. He urged me to come home and said you needed me.'

'He is right, your father's memory is failing.' She shook her head sadly. 'It started a couple of years after you left. At first it was innocuous things—he would search for hours for his spectacles, have the whole household involved, until eventually we would find them with the plants for potting in the greenhouse, secreted in one of the terracotta pots. Only he could have put them there, but he denied it vehemently.'

Richard nodded, but he was unable to imagine his once sharp father doing such a thing.

'It only got worse from there. He began forgetting the servants' names, at first those who were new to their positions, but after a while he struggled with everyone except those who have been here for decades. We would have conversations and a minute later he would be asking the same questions again, as if he hadn't heard a word I had said.'

'And now?' Richard asked, hardly wanting to hear the answer.

Lady Digby grimaced and closed her eyes for a moment before continuing. 'Now he has good days and bad days, but most of the time he is not in the present time. He asks for his mother and gets distressed when he doesn't recognise the faces of the servants. His physical health is failing, too, his appetite has gone and he becomes frail and sometimes...' She trailed off.

'Sometimes?' Richard prompted.

'Sometimes he doesn't even know who I am.' She

pressed her lips together in an effort to maintain composure.

'What does the doctor say?'

'Doctor Griffiths tells me your father is only going to get worse. Over the next few months, he will turn into little more than an infant in his behaviour and will become more distressed and disorientated.'

'I am sorry, Mother. What a burden you have had to bear.'

'I do not mind caring for him. We have had a wonderful life together and he has given me so much. I just hate to see him lose his dignity. Sometimes he becomes so distressed he is a danger to himself and I have to ask the footmen to hold him down until he calms. It is terrible to witness.'

She sank back into her chair, looking completely exhausted.

'What help do you have?'

For a moment her face lit up. 'We have the most dedicated servants. Your father's valet is a young man who is very calm and very strong and both our footmen are willing to help if needed, but our angel is Rose.'

'Rose?'

'Yes, the sweetest, most even-tempered young woman I have ever met. She has so much patience, so much understanding. Without Rose I truly do not know what I would do.' She beamed at him and then her expression grew serious. 'Do not do *anything* to upset Rose. We cannot cope without her.'

'Is she a companion? A nurse?'

'No, neither of those things. She worked as a nanny before she came to us, but she has no formal training.'

Lady Digby tilted her head to listen as the front door opened and closed again. 'That will be her now. She popped into St Ives for me to fetch a few things for your father.' She stood, crossing to the door and calling out, 'Rose, do come in. I want you to meet my son.'

Richard stood, a smile already on his face for the woman who seemed to take much of the burden from his mother. She glided into the room, a parcel in her hands and obscuring her face, but when she lowered it, Richard almost called out in surprise.

'You?'

Standing in front of him was the young woman from the bridge in St Ives, the one he had accused of trying to pick his pocket. There was a flicker of disdain on her face, but it was quickly hidden.

'Lovely to meet you Mr Digby,' Rose said, dropping into a curtsy and bowing her head. 'Your mother has been most excited for your return.'

'Do you two know each other?' Lady Digby looked from Rose to Richard and back again.

'No,' Rose said quickly before he could speak. 'We bumped into one another in St Ives, that is all. I did not realise he was your son, though, Lady Digby.'

'I have been telling Richard what an angel you are, Rose.'

'You'll make me blush, Lady Digby.'

Richard frowned, wondering how this young woman had managed to ingratiate herself with his mother so completely.

A footman came into the room and bent to murmur something in Lady Digby's ear.

'Will you excuse me for a moment. Your father is

asking for me and will not move until he has seen me. I will be a few minutes at most.'

'Do you want me to go, Lady Digby?' Rose asked.

'No, stay here, talk to Richard. Then when I get back, we can discuss how best to reintroduce Richard to his father.'

There was a lengthy silence once Lady Digby had left the room, leaving Richard alone with Rose.

'I will go and put these packages away,' Rose said after a minute, spinning quickly.

'Wait. My mother told you to stay here.'

Rose eyed him distastefully. 'I'd rather not.'

'I'm hardly going to assault you.'

She raised her eyebrows, but didn't leave, instead moving to perch on the edge of one of the armchairs.

Rose felt his eyes on her, watching all the time. It had been a shock to see him here in her home and it reminded her that she could never get too comfortable. Meadow View might feel like her sanctuary, but it was not hers and she was there only for as long as she was useful.

'I must apologise for what happened on the bridge,' Mr Digby said, taking a seat opposite her.

'Go on, then.'

He blinked a few times and then suppressed a smile. 'I am sorry, Miss…'

'Carpenter.'

'I am sorry, Miss Carpenter, for accusing you of picking my pocket.'

'You should be careful what you say about people. An accusation from a man of your class is enough to send a woman like me to the gallows.'

She held his gaze, wondering how he would react. Soon she would let the matter drop, but first she wanted him to realise there were consequences to his actions. People's lives were ruined by less.

He opened his mouth to speak, but Lady Digby breezed back into the room.

'Have you become acquainted? I am so glad.'

'How is Lord Digby?' Rose said.

'Settled now, my dear. He needed to come in to get cleaned up for dinner, but he would not believe Mr Watkins and insisted he hear it from me.'

'I would like to see him, Mother,' Mr Digby said, a touch impatiently.

'Of course, dear, but perhaps not yet. What do you think, Rose?'

Rose was watching the son of her employers and saw the flicker of irritation on his face. He might have been raised in the kindest of environments with the most generous parents, but he still struggled when people said no to him. It also looked as though he didn't like the idea of his mother asking Rose for her opinion.

'Often, he is most settled mid-morning. I wonder if that might be the best time to reintroduce Mr Digby to him,' Rose said.

'You're suggesting I wait until tomorrow?'

'That is not so long,' she said, biting back the comment she had wanted to make about it having been eight years, so one more day should not matter.

Lady Digby placed a placating hand on her son's arm and Rose saw some of the irritation melt away. At least he respected his mother's opinion.

'I think Rose is right. Your father keeps odd hours

and the evening seems to be the worst time for his memory. Sometimes he becomes agitated, especially if he is out of his routine.'

'You think my visit will put him out of his routine?'

'Yes,' Rose answered quickly so Lady Digby didn't have to. She felt fiercely protective towards this woman who had taken her in when she'd been at her lowest ebb and treated her so kindly. 'I do not wish to cause offence, Mr Digby, but your arrival will agitate Lord Digby. Change does—whether it is something joyful or something sorrowful, it upsets him. We cannot stop that. What we can do is minimise the disruption by choosing the best time to announce these changes.'

She was certain if Lady Digby was not in the room Mr Digby would have some choice words about her lecture. Instead, he nodded curtly.

'In that case I think I will freshen up.'

'I do not mean to keep you from your father, my dear,' Lady Digby said.

Again his expression softened as he looked at his mother. 'I know. I suppose I was impatient to see him. I am aware I have no right given I have been away for so long, but I feel this urge to see he is safe and as well as can be expected.'

He sounded so reasonable when his words were not directed at her. Rose smiled blandly, aware her life had just become a little more difficult now she had another master trying to impose his will.

'Will you show Richard up to his room?' Lady Digby said to Rose. 'I must talk to cook about the meals for the week now Richard is home. The blue room is prepared for him.'

'Of course, Lady Digby.'

She left the room first, waiting for Mr Digby in the hall.

'It has only been eight years. I am sure I can find my way.'

'Lady Digby redecorated a few years ago—I understand all the bedrooms were redone. They may not be as you remember them.'

She walked briskly up the stairs, turning left along the long corridor. There were more portraits up here, stern men and their striking wives, as well as a few pallid children, stretching all the way back to the first Baron Digby four hundred years earlier.

'In here,' Rose said as she opened the door and stepped back, allowing Mr Digby past. He paused in front of her and for the first time she allowed herself to really look at him. He was still young and, despite the weariness around his eyes, he looked no more than thirty. He had short brown hair, neatly styled, and light blue eyes. It was a striking combination and Rose had to acknowledge that physically he was a very attractive man.

'Thank you,' he said and then reached out and caught her arm as she made to leave.

Rose felt her pulse quicken as she looked up into his eyes.

'I am sorry for earlier, Miss Carpenter,' he said, his voice sincere and his gaze unwavering. 'I thought I felt your hand in my jacket and I was wrong. It was a terrible thing to accuse you of and you are right, I need to be more aware of the consequences of my words.'

For a moment Rose was speechless. She had assumed he was haughty and rude and that any apology was insincere. People of his social status rarely apologised to their servants, but here he was saying the words and actually meaning them.

'Thank you,' she said. He still held on to her forearm, his touch light, and Rose felt the inexplicable urge to stay there for a moment longer although the sensible thing to do would be to curtsy and walk away.

After ten seconds he let go, allowing her arm to drop gently back to her side. Then, without another word, he turned and walked into the bedroom, closing the door behind him.

Chapter Three

Rose woke in the night, unsettled. She was a light sleeper, a remnant from the time she had spent on the streets of London. It could be fatal to allow yourself to sleep deeply when there were dangers lurking in the shadows.

When she had first arrived at Meadow View she had been given a room on the top floor with the rest of the servants, but as Lord Digby's trust in her grew, and his health declined, Lady Digby had moved her to a small room that abutted theirs. There was a similar arrangement on the other side with Lord Digby's valet, meaning there was always someone close by in the event of a night-time wakening.

Her room now was beautiful. The walls were covered in cream wallpaper, decorated with delicate flowers of pink and yellow. The bed was comfortable and there was even room for an armchair and writing desk. Rosa felt lucky to have a sanctuary of her own, even though she knew it could all be taken away from her in one swoop.

Rising up out of bed, she pulled on her dressing gown and picked up the small clock from her mantelpiece. It was too dark to see the time so she crossed to the window and pulled back the curtains, allowing the moonlight in. It was a little after three o'clock, the quietest time of the night.

Stepping softly, Rose moved to the door that led into Lord and Lady Digby's bedroom, opening it a crack and peering in. She didn't want to intrude if they were both sleeping peacefully, but equally it was her job to check Lord Digby did not require anything. For a moment, she watched the two still figures in the bed, listening to the heavy, even breathing.

Once she had satisfied herself that Lord Digby was not disturbed, she quietly closed the door again and contemplated returning to bed. Her mouth was dry and she knew she would have difficulty getting back to sleep without first fetching a glass of water.

The hall was in complete darkness as she padded along it, shivering as her bare feet made contact with the polished wooden floorboards. This was not her first middle-of-the-night foray downstairs, and she made sure she avoided the creaky steps on the way down.

She liked Meadow View—it was by far the grandest house she had ever been in, but somehow it was still homely. Much of that was thanks to Lady Digby's influence, her skills at fostering a warm and happy atmosphere, but the rooms were well designed and the furniture comfortable, too.

Rose paused before she reached the stairs that led down to the kitchen, her eye caught by a flicker of light under one of the doorways. Her heart leaped in her chest. Fire was a real risk in grand households—all it needed for the devastation of a blaze to rip through a house was for one candle to be left lit unattended or a spark from a fire that had not been put out properly.

The light under the door was faint, though, and she thought it more likely from a candle than the start of a raging fire. Before she could talk herself out of it, she gripped the door handle and opened the door, feeling a flood of relief as she wasn't consumed by red-hot flames.

'You have a certain way of arriving in a room, Miss Carpenter,' Mr Digby said from his position in the chair behind the desk in his father's study.

She bristled, then saw the smile tugging at the corner of his lips. He was teasing her. It was a rare moment of light-heartedness and she wondered if this was what he had once been like before he had been driven away by whatever tragedy had forced him to flee England.

'I saw a light and I was afraid the room was on fire.'

'Then I must commend you for your swift actions. If the house was ablaze, then we would have a greater chance of saving it.'

'You mock me?' She was uncertain, not yet used to the tone of his voice.

'No, I am deadly serious. I have seen the devastation of fire. Anyone who is sensible enough to be vigilant for the beginning of a blaze holds a higher place in my regard.'

Rose hesitated, but she was curious about this man. She had heard so much of his past from Lady Digby, but snippets only. She suspected it was the happy parts, the parts Lady Digby enjoyed recalling. There was much she didn't know about him.

In the past few years there had been a few letters to his parents, telling them of the new country he had moved to, of the work he was occupying himself with. It was a fascinating way to live, but Rose suspected there was more to his self-imposed exile than a desire to help those less fortunate. He could do that while allowing himself to visit his loved ones once every few years.

'You have seen the devastation of fire?' Rose said, taking another step into the room.

'Yes. There was a terrible fire that destroyed numerous neighbourhoods after the earthquake in Caracas in 1812.'

'You were there?'

'Not at the time. I travelled there when I heard the news from neighbouring Colombia.'

These were places Rose had heard mentioned, but the idea of them seemed unfathomable. She could hardly imagine what they would be like with the blazing sun and the tropical heat. Some of the books she had borrowed from Lord Digby's library had described such places and the animals and people who lived in them, but she found it hard to imagine somewhere so different to the few places she had travelled in her lifetime. Rose ruefully shook her head. In her circumstances she was unlikely to ever visit France or Italy let alone somewhere exotic like Caracas.

'You are well travelled, Mr Digby.'

'Yes,' he said, his expression serious once again. 'I am.' There was a hint of regret in his voice, and she wondered if he was thinking about all the things he had missed out on while he had been away. 'It is the middle of the night, Miss Carpenter—what are you doing up?'

'I am a light sleeper and a noise woke me. Once I was awake I realised I needed a glass of water.'

'I am sorry if I disturbed you.'

'And you? Do you often sit up through the night?' It was an impertinent question for a maid to ask her master, but Mr Digby just smiled sadly.

'I have terrible insomnia. I have since…' He trailed off, then shook his head before continuing. 'Some nights I lie in bed tossing and turning, but often I find it better to get up, to occupy my mind for a time. Then when I return to bed sometimes I am lucky enough to sleep for a few hours.'

Rose looked at him a little closer and saw the weariness on his face. Earlier she had thought it was because of his long and arduous journey, but now she wasn't so sure. Lady Digby had never told her why her son had left, although there was always talk among the staff. Rose knew how devastating gossip could be so she tried not to listen, but she had picked up there was some sort of tragic event and Mr Digby had left in a hurry afterwards.

'I cannot imagine not being able to sleep.'

'It is unpleasant. To be awake when everyone else is slumbering and to know that your body is getting wearier and wearier, but your mind will not allow you to drift off.'

'Is there not a remedy, something the doctors can do?'

'No,' he said shortly, not deigning to explain if he had tried all the solutions put forward by the physicians or if he had not ever consulted them, but her instinct told her it was the latter. It was a curious situation and she found herself edging forward, further into the room. She wanted to know what had made this man flee to the other side of the world, what was so terrible that he suffered sleepless nights all these years on.

Mr Digby stood and stretched and walked towards her. Rose felt her pulse quickening as she remembered another night a few years earlier, a similar situation. Her master then had often stayed up late and every night would invite her to take a drink with him. For six months every night she had refused, knowing where it would lead, but after receiving some bad news one evening she had relented.

For a moment she was back at Thetford House, backing away from her old master as he approached her with a glint of possessiveness in his eyes. She felt the rise of nausea, the knowledge that, whatever she did, nothing would ever be the same again.

She must have started for Mr Digby paused a few feet away, looking at her with a curious expression.

'Is something amiss, Miss Carpenter?'

'Sorry,' she said quickly, her eyes flicking over his face. There was nothing predatory there, nothing that hinted at desire, and she felt a wave of shame flood through her. 'I am tired, that is all. I will bid you goodnight. I hope you get some sleep, Mr Digby.'

Walking slowly so she could tell herself she was not fleeing, she left the study and went to the kitchen, hating how her hand shook, and she took a glass from the high shelf.

Over and over she reminded herself that she was safe,

that this was her home and no one could hurt her in it, yet she knew deep down that wasn't true.

Feeling unsettled, she returned to bed, not stopping this time as she passed the study.

Chapter Four

It felt like the first day of school as he stood outside his father's room. He had a ball of nerves in his stomach and the impulse to keep fiddling with his cravat.

The door opened and Miss Carpenter slipped out, her pretty face set into a smile that didn't quite reach her eyes. She was a curious woman, confident for someone so young and in a position of service, yet in the study last night he had seen uncertainty in her expression.

'Your father slept well,' she said, biting her lip, 'But he has struggled with the idea of getting dressed today.'

'I see.'

'Your mother has managed to calm him, but I do not think we are going to persuade him out of his nightshirt.'

'Does this often happen?'

'In truth? Yes, more and more.'

'I suppose it is a case of picking your battles.'

'It is.'

Richard took a deep, steadying breath, reminding himself of all the challenges he had faced over the last eight years. None of them seemed as gargantuan as facing the truth of how his father had changed.

Miss Carpenter opened the door and led him into the room. Years earlier, soon after his father had inherited Meadow View, Lord and Lady Digby had decided to do away with the traditional separated but interconnected bedrooms and instead used one of the rooms as a private sitting room. It meant they had a cosy suite, with the bedroom connected to the sitting room that allowed them privacy and space at the same time.

This arrangement was ideal now, for his father could comfortably exist mainly in the two rooms without too many concerns about how he might injure himself as he might if he was free to wander around the whole house.

'Henry darling,' Lady Digby said. She sat in an armchair next to her husband, holding his hand. 'Richard is back. Our son, Richard, he is back from his travels.'

Richard felt as though his shoes were filled with the densest of metals as he tried to make his way across the room. He had the urge to turn away, to retreat, but he knew it was not an option. Instead, he forced a smile on his face as he came to face his father.

'Richard?' Lord Digby said. 'Where is he?'

'I am here, Father,' Richard said, crouching down. For a long moment the old man's eyes searched his own as if looking for something familiar there. Richard felt himself holding his breath, willing the old man to smile in recognition, to make a joke or pull him into an embrace.

'Where is my son?' Lord Digby said.

'I am here, Father.'

Lord Digby looked again, frowning, and then shook his head. 'My boy is young. You are a man.'

Richard felt as though he had been stabbed through the heart and he saw a similar pain cross his mother's face.

'This is Richard, my darling,' she said, calm and patient. 'He has been away a while, do you remember? He has been travelling the world.'

'Richard is a boy,' Lord Digby said.

'He was a boy,' Lady Digby said softly. 'He has grown now and he's here to see you.'

Richard didn't know what he would do if his father rejected him completely, but to his relief the old man nodded quite reasonably.

'He's been away,' he murmured. 'He's grown up.'

'Yes, that's right, Father. I've been away.'

'Come and sit with me, my boy.'

Richard pulled a chair over and sat next to his father, trying not to show the devastation that he felt inside. His father had always been so vibrant, so full of life. His mind had been quick and lively, making connections before anyone else could. This man looked like his father, he spoke in the same voice and held his head in the same way, but there was something scared behind his eyes, something that showed he was desperately trying to grasp at the threads of memories.

'How are you?' Richard asked, seeing his mother relax back a little into her chair.

'Damn tired of all this fussing. All I want to do is go to my glasshouse, but no one will let me out. I am a prisoner in my own home.'

'You can go to your glasshouse later, my dear,' Lady Digby said, her voice soothing. 'Once you are dressed.'

'I am dressed,' Lord Digby said, looking down at his nightshirt. 'Is the King visiting? Are we off to court? I hardly need to be in my smartest jacket and cravat.'

'No, dear,' his mother said. 'You are right.'

Lord Digby turned to Richard, frowning. 'Who are you?'

'It is Richard, Father.'

'No, my Richard is a boy.'

Richard pressed his lips together and nodded reassuringly at his mother. It was devastating to see his father like this, but he knew the importance of keeping calm. He mirrored the reassuring tone Lady Digby had used and steered the conversation away from his identity.

The conversation was circular. Over and over his father would repeat the same questions, give the same pieces of information. At one point he became quite agitated, calling out for his mother, and Richard marvelled at the calm way Miss Carpenter stepped in, telling his father she would go and look for his mother now.

After half an hour his father announced abruptly he wanted to rest and stood, holding out his hand for Richard to shake. As Richard left the room he heard Lord Digby ask his wife who the nice man was and why they hadn't been introduced.

He had the sudden urge to get outside, to shake off the oppressive warmth of the room and breathe in big gulps of fresh air. Walking briskly, he made his way downstairs and out of the house, not stopping until he was in the middle of the rose garden where he sank down on to the wall of the small fountain that trickled in the middle.

He closed his eyes, trying to tell himself it could be so much worse, but in reality he could not see how. His father did not recognise him, not at all. At some point in the last eight years his essence, his personality and all his memories had slipped away and Richard had not been here. He had lost the chance to say goodbye, to hold his father's hand while he still remembered, to tell him that he had been the best of fathers.

Richard felt a surge of grief and anger and he stood, needing to take that anger out on something. There was nothing at all suitable nearby and after scuffing his boots against the wall of the fountain a few times he let out a deep bellow of frustration.

'Shall I come back later, sir?' The calm voice of Miss Carpenter came from between the roses.

'Were you creeping up on me?'

He saw her bristle and knew he was being unfair, letting his anger and feelings of powerlessness making him lash out.

'No,' she said shortly. 'Your mother asked me to check on you. Lord Digby is settled and resting and your mother has decided to have a lie down herself.'

Richard frowned. There was something in the way the young woman spoke that felt like an accusation.

'My mother asked you to check on me?'

'Yes.' She cleared her throat and stepped closer. 'That cannot have been easy.'

He gave a mirthless laugh. 'I would rather have suffered a hundred lashes than have to see my father like that.'

'He is comfortable, Mr Digby, and he is well cared for. I know it does not sound like much, but he is so very lucky to have your mother. She is always thinking of his dignity, his safety, and she makes sure he does not suffer.' Richard knew she was only trying to be helpful, to reassure him, but he felt like hitting out. He wanted to ask her what she truly knew about it, whether she had seen someone she loved spiral into this type of madness, but he knew it was an unreasonable reaction.

Instead, he remained quiet and sat back down on the wall of the fountain, looking into the water, dark under the lily pads.

He was surprised when she came to sit next to him. There was a good foot between them and no question of impropriety, but it was a strange thing for a maid to do and he found himself wondering about this woman's background. His mother had said her last post was as a nanny and, now he had seen his father and the coaxing and cajoling needed to get him to do the essential everyday things, he could see how her previous experience might help.

'I wonder if I might speak plainly, Mr Digby?'

He regarded her for a long moment and then nodded, wondering what fresh burden she was going to place at his door.

'Lady Digby is exhausted. These past few months have not been easy on her. She has had no break, no respite. Most nights her sleep is disturbed, but she still sleeps beside your father and every day there is some new worry to occupy her.'

Richard tried not to take Miss Carpenter's words as an accusation, but his own guilt at letting his mother bear this burden alone welled up inside him and he knew if he was not careful he might let it cloud his judgement.

'I can see her weariness.'

'Are you here to stay, sir?'

It was a big question, one Richard did not know the answer to. When he had left England eight years ago he had been fleeing from a crime and a tragedy, and at that point he had thought he would never come back. Over time he had realised one day his return might be possible, but he had not ever felt as though he deserved it. His guilt had kept him away and, once he had helped his mother through this awful time, he suspected it would drive him far away again.

'For now.'

'For how long?'

'Miss Carpenter, I hardly think it is any of your concern.'

'Forgive me,' she said, sounding completely unrepentant. 'I only mean to speak for my mistress.'

'Lady Digby has a voice of her own. She does not need you to speak for her.'

'She is dedicated to your father, but if she continues much longer she will collapse. She needs a rest, Mr Digby, a break, so she can recuperate, but also so she can prepare herself for what is to come.'

Richard frowned. He could see the exhaustion in his mother's eyes.

'A break?'

'Yes. Even a few days would be something.'

He looked out into the distance, across the roses and

to the grass beyond where it sloped gently down to the River Great Ouse.

'My father would find the change unsettling.'

'He would, but better to have a short, planned break now than for your mother to be overcome with exhaustion in a month or two. She needs her strength and her health.'

Loath as he was to admit it, he could see Miss Carpenter was probably right. His mother had been shouldering this burden for so long that it had to be weighing her down. He was no expert in looking after his father, but he could ensure the smooth running of the household and the keeping of the routine while his mother recuperated.

'I will speak to Lady Digby,' he said.

'Thank you.'

Miss Carpenter stood and began to walk away, but he called out before she had taken more than five steps.

'Stay a moment, Miss Carpenter. I wish to know a little more about you.'

Her saw her expression cloud with apprehension and her eyes narrowed just a fraction.

'What do you wish to know?'

'You seem very experienced in looking after my father—have you done this sort of work before?'

'Not exactly, but I helped to look after my guardian. A few years ago his health began failing and with it his mind. It was different to your father, but I learned a little of what works and what does not.'

'Is he still with us?'

'No, he passed away four years ago.'

'I am sorry to hear that.'

'Thank you.'

'You are from London, I think?'

Miss Carpenter gave a rueful smile. 'Is my accent that obvious?'

'Yes. Do you have family there still?'

She shifted again and looked over her shoulder. 'I should get back, Mr Digby.' Before he could protest she turned and hurried away. Richard watched her go. There was something intriguing about the way Miss Carpenter was so vague about her past.

He understood the desire to live in the present without dwelling on past events, but most people did not mind making small talk about their families or their origins. She seemed jumpy around him as well. He had noticed it the night before, the way she had backed away as he had approached. There was a wariness in her eyes that made him wonder if someone had hurt this young woman at some point in her life.

With a sigh, he put the topic from his mind. He knew he was desperately grasping for something to occupy his thoughts other than the terrible state his father was in.

Chapter Five

Rose raised her hand and waved at the carriage, a genuine smile on her lips even though she knew the next week would be harder without Lady Digby's presence. Rose had experienced her fair share of scoundrels and wastrels throughout her life, but she had known truly kind people as well. Lady Digby was one of the kind ones.

Rose's suggestion she take a few days to herself had not been entirely selfless. Rose and Mr Watkins did much of the physical aspects of Lord Digby's care, but Lady Digby was his emotional support, his one constant. There would be much disruption while she was away, but at least Mr Digby would be there to shoulder some of the burden.

She'd suggested the idea for her mistress to have a few days' rest as soon as possible for she wasn't sure how long Mr Digby would stay. He had a haunted look about his eyes and every so often she caught him staring out of the window as if wishing he was somewhere else.

Mr Watkins came hurrying from the house, concern etched on his heavy features.

'Miss Carpenter,' he said, his voice low, 'we have a problem.'

'A problem?'

'Lord Digby became a little distressed when he saw Lady Digby get into the carriage. He broke free from his rooms and made a dash through the house.'

'Where is he now, Mr Watkins?'

'Running round the garden, Miss Carpenter.'

'Is there a problem?' Mr Digby said.

Rose exhaled slowly. 'Nothing we cannot handle, Mr Digby.'

He gave her an assessing look and then took a step closer.

'I think we need to discuss what is going to happen while my mother is away, Miss Carpenter.'

'Certainly, sir,' she said, clenching her jaw to bite back the harsher words she wished she could say. 'Although perhaps it could wait until we have your father back in the safety of his rooms.'

'Where is he, Miss Carpenter?'

'In the gardens.'

Mr Digby moved quickly, and Rose had to almost run to keep up. They rounded the side of the house together, Mr Watkins a few paces behind. Lord Digby was nowhere to be seen at first glance and Rose felt her heart sinking. The last thing they needed was to start the time with Lady Digby away with a farcical chase around the grounds of Meadow View.

She saw a flash of colour and some movement out of the corner of her eye and spun quickly, taking off down the garden towards the river. Behind her, she heard Mr Digby following and she hoped the rest of the servants would have the sense to fan out through the gardens and block off any routes of escape.

'He's heading for the river,' Mr Digby said as he ran past her, jacket tails flapping behind him.

Rose felt her heart sink. The river was not fast flowing here, but it was deep and at this time of year there was a bloom of underwater plants that could tangle Lord Digby's feet and pull him to the bottom. That was assuming he could swim, which wasn't guaranteed even with living in such close proximity to the water.

'Father, stop,' Mr Digby said as they neared the end of the garden.

Lord Digby was on the bank now, teetering wildly, his eyes fixed on the far side of the river.

'I need to get out.'

'Stop, you're going to fall in the water.'

Lord Digby ignored his son, taking another step down the bank. Thankfully, they had not had any rain recently and the ground was dry, otherwise he would have slid into the water.

Rose came to a halt a few feet away. She felt a deep dread. Water scared her. Growing up in London, she had never learned to swim, never had the opportunity. Here in Cambridgeshire, she would sometimes see the young people jumping from the banks of the river in the summer, confident and carefree, but the thought of something pulling her into its murky depths was too much for her.

'What are you doing, Lord Digby?' Rose asked, her voice calm and gentle. She moved slowly, trying not to show her true emotions.

'I need my Penelope,' Lord Digby said, taking another step to the water. 'I can't find her and those people are keeping her from me.'

Mr Digby went to speak, but Rose held up a hand, ignoring the indignant look on his face. She couldn't have him blundering in and saying the wrong thing, not with such a delicate matter. If he wanted to be angry with her later then so be it—she would put her master's safety before Mr Digby's pride.

'Penelope is coming back soon,' she said, her voice soothing. 'She asked if you would wait for her in the glasshouse, she wishes to see what you have been planting.'

'My Penelope is coming back?'

'Yes, she will only be a few minutes. Shall we get you to the glasshouse, so you are there waiting for her?'

'They said she had gone,' Lord Digby said, turning his confused eyes to Rose.

'They were wrong. Come, take my hand and we will get you ready to see your Penelope.'

Rose let out a shaky breath as Lord Digby turned away from the water and took a step up the bank. She kept her eyes locked on the old man's, knowing he found reassurance in them.

'What are we going to do when he realises she isn't coming back?' Mr Digby murmured in her ear.

'Distraction is a very powerful tool.'

'Someone said my boy was coming home, my Richard. He's off at school, you know. He's a strapping lad.'

'I cannot wait to meet him, my lord,' Rose said, reaching out for the old man's hand. The two footmen had arrived now, although had the good sense not to crowd in.

Lord Digby gripped her hand and smiled at her and Rose felt her heart squeeze in her chest. There was trepidation in his eyes and she knew he was having a moment of near lucidity where everything he was experiencing seemed so petrifying.

One of the footmen shifted a little and Lord Digby turned quickly, startled by the movement. He was still holding on to Rose's hand, his knuckles turning white as he gripped her firmly.

Rose felt him topple and lose his balance, his free arm trying to grab at the air to steady himself. He was still on the slope of the bank, not yet on safe ground, and as he began to slip Rose lost her balance, too, tumbling with him.

Mr Digby lunged for them. As Rose slipped towards the water, she felt Lord Digby wrenched away as his son caught him by his shirt and pulled him to safety.

Without the weight of Lord Digby pulling her backwards, for a moment Rose thought she might be able to save herself from the water, but it was too little, too late, and with a scream she fell from the bank. There was a big splash and instantly Rose plunged under the water.

She panicked, feeling the weight of the water as it soaked into the heavy material of her dress, trying to drag her down. Desperately, she kicked for the surface, her head breaking free long enough for her to take a gulp of air before the water closed over her head again.

In her terror, Rose couldn't think straight. Her lungs burned in her chest and her vision darkened. She had this urge to open her mouth, to take in a mouthful of water, but she knew if she did that it would be the end of her.

Her feet struck the bottom of the riverbed and she tried to push up, but she was becoming disorientated. It was dark in the water and she couldn't see more than a foot in front of her as the murky river water stung her eyes.

She let out the last puff of air as strong arms gripped her, pulling her upwards. She gasped as they broke through the surface of the water, petrified they would sink again, but this time her head stayed above the water and she was able to take in a few shuddering breaths.

'Kick,' Mr Digby urged her, his lips close to her ear.

Rose didn't react for a moment, so he spun her to face him in the water.

'Miss Carpenter, I need you to kick.'

This time she obeyed, kicking her legs and cursing her skirt every time her legs got caught.

They were only a few feet from the bank, although they had travelled a little downstream, but within ten seconds Mr Digby had propelled her to the bank, holding her steady as the footmen and Mr Watkins pulled her out. Rose lay panting on the grass, her head pounding and her heart hammering in her chest. Beside her she was vaguely aware of Mr Digby pulling himself from the water and collapsing on to the riverbank.

Rose struggled to sit up. She felt nauseous, but she needed to see Lord Digby was unharmed. She did not think he had entered the river, too, but she wanted to see for herself. He was standing a good way back from the bank, the two footmen by his side in case he decided he would like to assist in the rescue attempt.

'Are you hurt, Miss Carpenter?' Mr Digby said. He was breathing heavily, but otherwise did not look too unsettled that he had just had to dive into a river to save her from drowning.

'No—at least, I do not think so.'

'Good. I am sorry, I could not reach you in time to stop you from falling in.'

Rose shivered despite the warmth of the day. Her clothes were stuck to her body and all she wanted to do was stand in front of a warm fire until she was dry.

'Thank you for coming to my aid.'

'You cannot swim.' It was said as a statement, but Mr Digby was looking at her curiously.

'No, there is not much opportunity to learn in London.'

'I suppose not.' He stood, looking down at his soaked clothes, and shook his head ruefully. 'Come, Miss Carpenter, we need to get undressed.'

She knew what he meant, but all the same she couldn't stop her eyes from raking over his body where his shirt stuck to his torso. Quickly, she forced herself to look away. Mr Digby was an attractive man, but the last thing she needed was for him to get the wrong idea about her because he caught her staring.

Allowing him to help her to her feet, Rose self-consciously adjusted her own dress before starting the walk up through the gardens. Mr Digby sent the other servants on ahead with his father and he kept his eyes averted, but Rose was acutely aware of the way her dress clung to her curves. In front of them, Lord Digby was ushered into the glasshouse by one of the footmen and Rose was pleased to see Mr Watkins go hurrying in to join them.

Before they entered the house, Mr Digby stopped her.

For one mad moment Rose thought he might ask her to take her clothes off outside so she did not drip through the hallways, but instead he stood in silence for a moment until she met his eye.

'I cannot imagine how traumatic that must have been if you cannot swim,' he said softly.

'I will be fine, Mr Digby.'

'I am sure you will, Miss Carpenter.' It was said with a half-smile and he held her eye for a moment. Rose felt a surge of warmth deep inside and had the sudden urge to reach out and take his hand.

Quickly, she stepped away before she could do anything inappropriate.

'I would like to see you once you have changed and cleaned yourself up, although I know your duties with my father come first. Perhaps you can come to my study after lunch and we can discuss how we are going to manage these next few days.'

'Of course, Mr Digby,' Rose said, her heart sinking. She might have been the one suggesting Lady Digby take a few days away, but it didn't mean she wanted Mr Digby upsetting their routine.

Chapter Six

Richard sat looking out the window, tapping his fingers on the arm of his chair. He was eager to get out, to leave the house and stride through the countryside, perhaps even ride out on horseback. His parents had always kept an enviable stable of horses and, even though it was a little depleted now, there were still plenty of fine animals to choose from for a leisurely ride.

He wasn't used to this sedate pace of life. For the last few years it was as though he had been driven by an invisible force, always pushing him to keep moving, to keep himself busy. He wasn't so naive to think this was entirely altruistic—the busier he kept himself, the less time his guilt had to fester and build.

If he was doing hard, physical labour from dawn until dusk, as soon as he stopped his body would be so exhausted he would collapse into bed, hopefully for a few hours of sleep at some point in the night. The exhaustion was his shield, his protection from the terrible thoughts in his head.

Here at Meadow View, it was impossible to escape

the serenity. Everything about life was slower and everything was designed to be calm and quiet so it would best suit Lord Digby, but it did mean he had far too much time to himself. Time in which his own thoughts were starting to take over.

There was a rap on the door and Miss Carpenter entered. She was dressed in a clean, dry dress, similar to the one that had been soaked in the river earlier in the day. It was dark grey in colour with long sleeves and a high neck despite the heat. It was demure, but not completely without shape, nipping in at the waist and flaring out over her hips.

'Lord Digby is having a rest,' Miss Carpenter said, hovering near the door.

'Come in, Miss Carpenter. How are you?'

She looked wary, and Richard realised she treated him completely differently to how she treated his mother. They were both in a position of power, both able to make decisions over her employment status, yet she was both cautious and defiant around him, whereas with his mother she was patient and caring.

'I am fine, thank you.'

'You do not feel unwell after your dip in the river?'

'No,' she said, but her hand flitted to her chest. He wondered if she had inhaled some water. The river was fast flowing and relatively clean, but if she had breathed some of the water deep into her lungs there was a chance of a serious infection.

'Good. Please take a seat, Miss Carpenter.'

She perched on the edge of an armchair, her posture stiff and a tension in her demeanour that made Richard wonder if she was preparing for a fight.

'We need to discuss how best we look after my father while Lady Digby is away.'

'I agree.'

'I am aware you have been here for quite some time and have a certain way of doing things.'

'A way that has been settled on through months of trial and error, of noting down what seems to work well and what does not.'

'I understand that, Miss Carpenter, but we also have to be adaptable.'

She inclined her head. 'Yes, adaptable,' she murmured as if reminding herself of the idea.

'I think if we stick to my father's normal routine he will notice my mother is gone, whereas if we change a few things then he will be more focused on the changes.'

'That is not wise, Mr Digby,' Miss Carpenter said, her voice clipped, and he could see she was holding something back.

'Go on.'

'Your father thrives on routine. It is the one thing, apart from Lady Digby, that keeps him feeling safe. Take away his routine and he is floundering.'

Richard regarded the young woman and considered her words. He could see her point, but he was concerned that if at four o'clock Lord Digby normally took tea with Lady Digby in the drawing room, if they kept to that routine and Lady Digby did not appear it would be distressing.

'I suggest a compromise,' he said, his tone firm. He wanted to show Miss Carpenter he was a reasonable man. He would listen to reason, but was not going to sit back and not be involved these next few weeks. 'We keep to the same general routine, but if there is something that normally heavily involves my mother, we avoid it.'

'Whatever you wish,' Miss Carpenter said, although there was a flicker of defiance in her eyes. Richard felt a mild irritation. No matter how good Miss Carpenter was with his father she was still just an employee, a paid servant who should be better at taking orders.

'I also need you to communicate with me. I do not want to have to find out my father has gone missing from the frantic looks the footmen are giving each other. My father is my responsibility and I need you to understand that.'

'I understand.' She said the words, but Richard felt as though she was just saying what she thought he wanted to hear.

'This is a matter I am insistent on, Miss Carpenter.'

She sighed, and he felt a surge of irritation, wondering if she was so rude to his mother. 'I will inform you of what is happening, Mr Digby, but it is not my priority. My priority is keeping your father happy and safe. Often that will mean I have to prioritise something I am doing with him over coming to speak to you.'

'I am not asking you to do that,' Richard said, his fingers gripping the edge of the chair.

'I am capable of doing my job, Mr Digby. Your mother trusts me. *I* have been here for a long time, looking after your father for a long time.'

'Tread carefully, Miss Carpenter.'

She pressed her lips together, but wisely did not say any more.

For a long moment they sat staring at each other, as

if waiting to see who would crack first. Richard could not believe the impertinence of the young woman and wondered if she spoke to his mother in the same way.

'I think we are done,' he said eventually, standing up to dismiss her. She turned without another word and left the room.

Rose was seething. She had known Mr Digby would assert his dominance at some point, but she hadn't thought it would be so soon after she had been pulled into the river. It was irritating to be told what to do by a man who had not even been in the country these last few years. She was dedicated to the Digbys—she knew how much she owed Lady Digby for taking her in at her moment of need, and she was fiercely loyal. It stung to be told by a man who had all but abandoned his family how she should be doing things.

Rose was aware she was possibly being unfair. She didn't know all the details, but she did know how much Lady Digby had suffered here on her own. Rose had tried her hardest to alleviate some of that suffering and now she was being ordered to report her movements to a man who had not, in her eyes, earned the right to ask it of her.

Slowly, she exhaled. Her temper had often got her into trouble when she was a girl and it had been a reason she had bounced from place to place when she was younger. She had never been awed by authority, never felt the need to bow and scrape to those who had been born more fortunate than herself.

When her guardians had taken her in and given her a home they had been careful not to crush her spirit, aware it had been one of the things that had kept her alive and fighting for so long. They had, however, shown her the importance of control. Now most of the time she didn't let slip exactly what she was thinking, although she knew sometimes her expression left a lot to be desired.

'Miss Carpenter,' called out Mrs Green, the jovial cook at Meadow View. 'Why don't you come and join me for a cup of tea if you have a minute?'

Rose hesitated, but the draw of the cosy kitchen was too great to ignore. She loved it down in the vaulted rooms, loved the smells and sounds, the bustle and the friendly camaraderie between the cook and the maids. Mrs Green had been at Meadow View for decades and, as with all the servants, she had been carefully chosen by Lady Digby for not only her culinary ability, but also her kind nature.

Mrs Green led Rose into the small room off to one side of the large kitchen and set about pouring tea.

'You did well, my dear,' the older woman said as she sat down opposite her. 'Persuading Lady Digby to take a few days away.'

Rose sighed. 'I think she was near to breaking point.'

'Yes, it is a burden, but at least Mr Digby is home now.'

Rose let out a strangled grunt of acknowledgement that had Mrs Green smiling. 'You are not enamoured with the young master, I take it?'

Rose closed her eyes for a second and took a sip of tea, allowing some of the tension to seep from her. It felt safe down here in the kitchens and she knew Mrs Green would never betray her confidence by repeating any of what she said here.

'I think his intentions are good,' she said eventually.
Mrs Green chuckled. 'But his execution is not.'

'He has been away for so long, yet he acts as though
he knows best. He is so superior and stern, but he has
not a clue about what his father actually needs.'

'You must show him, my dear. Guide him, lead him.
Put yourself in his shoes. He's been away for eight years
and he returns to find the father he loved so deeply a
vastly changed man. Now the person who once guided
him, advised him, needs to be cared for like a vulnerable child. Of course he feels uncertain.'

'He could just ask for help,' Rose muttered.

'Yes, he could, but it is not how men of his class are
raised. They go off to those terrible schools and are
taught to show no emotion, to never ask for help. Mr
Digby at least had his parents to counter that message,
but it is hard to break what you are taught.'

'Why did he stay away for so long?'

Mrs Green hesitated, then shook her head. 'It is not
my story to tell. Something tragic happened and Mr
Digby blamed himself.'

'So he ran away?' Rose was aware she was being un-
charitable, but she could not imagine what could keep
a man away from his family for so long. She shook her
head. 'Don't answer that.'

'People deal with adversity in different ways. Sometimes it feels as though the only way to keep those you
love safe is to remove yourself from the situation.'

Rose fell silent and took a sip of her tea. It was sweet
and hot and just what she needed right now. She could
acknowledge the jealousy that swirled through her emotions. She had never had the chances that Mr Digby had,

and until she was ten years old, she had not known what unconditional love was. Mr Digby had grown up with two parents who cared for him, loved him, cherished him, yet he had still abandoned them.

'Perhaps you should ask him about it yourself,' Mrs Green said quietly.

With an unladylike snort, Rose shook her head. 'I do not think we will ever have that sort of relationship.'

'Give him time. Remember what he has come home to.'

Rose finished her tea in silence, mulling over the cook's words. Perhaps she was being too harsh on the man. She refused to put his wants above her duty to care for Lord Digby, but she could probably find a way to balance everything a little better.

Chapter Seven

Rose sat bolt upright, woken suddenly by the loud clatter from the room next door. She sprang out of bed, wide awake instantly and moving across the room with her arms stretched out in front of her. It was completely black, that darkest part of the night when sunrise was still hours away. There was no moon tonight to shine through the gap in the curtains, and Rose stumbled a couple of times before her hands found the door-handle.

Lord Digby was up, wandering about the room, looking distressed. He didn't notice Rose enter, but he did look up when Mr Watkins came in through the other door to the room.

'Stay away,' Lord Digby said, grasping the back of a chair as if he was thinking of brandishing it at his valet.

Mr Watkins glanced at her, and Rose nodded, her heart pounding in her chest. These night-time awakenings were becoming more and more common. Lord Digby would be more confused in the evenings and overnight too, often regressing back years in his mind.

'Who are you?' he said, his eyes fixed on Mr Watkins.

'Come, my lord, let us get you to bed. It is late and you must be tired.' Rose took a step forward, then another.

When she was about three feet away the door to the room opened again and she heard Mr Digby's low voice asking Mr Watkins what had happened. Rose ignored them, focused solely on the man in front of her.

'Where is my mother? I need to see her this instant,' Lord Digby said. His eyes fixed on her, pleading like a child's.

'Your mother is coming,' Rose said, her voice firm but kind. 'She wants you to get back into bed and when you are settled she will come and sing to you like she did when you were young.'

'My mother has the best singing voice.'

'I know. Come, take my hand. Let us get you settled.'

The fear slowly faded from his eyes, and Rose reached out, guiding him back to bed. She saw Mr Digby shift uncomfortably as she perched beside the old man. She was aware she had not had time to get her dressing gown and wore only a thin cotton nightdress, but there was nothing to be done about it now.

As if she were looking after a child, she plumped Lord Digby's pillow and then tucked him in, smiling as he gripped her hand. Then softly she began to sing.

It took half an hour for the old man to settle and fall back into a peaceful slumber, and Rose remained still for another ten minutes to make sure she did not rouse him when she moved. At some point, Mr Digby and Mr Watkins had left, moving from the room silently so they did not cause a disturbance.

Rose felt stiff as she stood, but despite her tiredness she had a warm glow inside her. She liked being able to settle Lord Digby when he was distressed. She did not know what awful depths his mind plunged to, but the fear she saw in his eyes sometimes was real and devastating. It felt good to be able to help assuage that fear.

'Miss Carpenter,' Mr Digby whispered as she left the room. Rose jumped. She had thought he had gone back to bed. 'I made you a drink.'

She paused, surprised, as he brandished a cup of warm milk at her. It was an odd thing for anyone to do, let alone a man for his servant.

'Thank you.'

'Join me?'

Rose was wide awake and aware she would not get much more sleep that night, so she nodded, wondering what Mr Digby wanted with her at four in the morning.

As they walked downstairs, Rose realised she probably should have picked up her dressing gown, but they were already nearing Lord Digby's study. Inside, there were four candles flickering, just enough to illuminate the room. Mr Digby waited for her to sit and then handed her the cup.

The milk was warm and sweet and comforting and Rose closed her eyes as she took her first sip.

'It is a peace offering,' Mr Digby said at length. 'I realise I came across poorly this afternoon.' He paused, his eyes fixed on her. 'You were very good with my father in there. I would not...' He trailed off.

'You would not have known what to do?' Rose concluded.

'No.'

Silently, Rose nodded, feeling some of the irritation she held towards Mr Digby drain away.

'I was an ass earlier. Pompous. Can you forgive me?'

'There is nothing to forgive,' Rose said, thinking it was what was expected of her.

'There is. I promise I am not normally this insufferable. I find myself…' he searched for the right word for a few seconds '…adrift. I am aware I have no real role in this situation. My mother has done an excellent job of managing without me. She has surrounded herself with capable, caring people, from you to Mr Watkins, even to the footmen who are sympathetic to my father's illness. I am not *needed*.'

'You may not be needed to fulfil a practical role, Mr Digby,' Rose said softly, 'but that does not mean your presence isn't important.'

He shook his head and Rose saw the devastation in his eyes. She thought of Mrs Green's words earlier in the day and forced herself to imagine what it would be like coming home to find the father you had once loved didn't even recognise you.

'I have been at Meadow View for two years, Mr Digby—in all that time your mother has not once taken a break. I have urged her to rest, to visit her sister as she is now, to take a few days so she might come back healthier and able to cope with what is to come, but she has always delayed. Yet you return and within a few days she feels comfortable enough to leave.'

Rose leaned forward, having to resist the urge to reach out and take Mr Digby's hand. 'Do not underestimate the reassurance just being here can give. You do not have to be the one to soothe your father back to sleep or ensure he eats his meals—that is not your role. You need to have an overview of everything, making sure the whole household runs smoothly.'

Mr Digby looked suddenly tired, but he smiled at her. 'You are very persuasive, Miss Carpenter. If life was fair you would have a position in Parliament—I think you would be very influential.' He leaned back in his chair, his eyes still locked on hers. 'I do not wish to be at odds with you, Miss Carpenter. I can see why my mother relies on you so heavily.'

'Now she has you to rely on, too.'

Rose shivered, wrapping her arms around her body. Even though the days were warm at this time of year, the nights still had a chill to them and she was missing the extra layer of her dressing gown.

'I am sorry, it was unforgivable, dragging you downstairs like this. You should get to bed, Miss Carpenter.'

'What about you?' As soon as she said the words, she felt her cheeks flush. Although innocent, she wondered if it sounded like an invitation to Mr Digby, and for a second she thought she saw a flicker of intrigue in his eyes. Rose hastily looked down, willing her heart to stop pounding in her chest.

'I will retire soon, Miss Carpenter.'

Rose stood and was surprised to find Mr Digby rise from his chair as well. He took one of the candles and held out his arm for her.

'Let me escort you upstairs.'

They walked side by side, their arms brushing against one another on a couple of occasions, but even when they did not touch, Rose was acutely aware of the man walking beside her. Her reaction to him was something she could not control, despite telling herself to stop being so foolish. As they came to her room, Mr Digby paused outside her door and Rose rested her hand on the door handle.

'Sleep well, Miss Carpenter,' Mr Digby said quietly.

'Thank you.'

Neither of them moved. Rose felt her chest rise and fall more rapidly as she glanced up at the man standing in front of her. He was looking straight at her and as their eyes met she felt a spark pass between them. It happened so fast she wondered if it was just a product of her overtired imagination, but then she saw the expression on Mr Digby's face and knew he had felt it, too.

He stepped back and bowed, then spun before Rose could say anything, leaving her feeling confused and surprised in equal measure.

Quickly, she fumbled for the door handle and entered her bedroom, closing the door with a soft click behind her. For a few seconds she rested her head on the cool wood of the door, trying to make sense of what had just happened.

'You're tired, that is all,' she murmured to herself.

The very last thing she needed was to develop an infatuation with Mr Digby. For two years at Meadow View she had experienced peace and it had been wonderful. She did not need any romantic complications in her life, even if it was nothing more than an impossible infatuation on her part. She had been hurt before by giving herself to someone she could not have a future with, someone who held his position of power over her. She would not make the same mistake twice.

Chapter Eight

The sun was shining, outside the birds were singing and he had even managed to sleep for a few hours. Today Richard could tell it was going to be a good day. He was glad of the late-night talk he had arranged with Miss Carpenter, even if it was a little unusual. It had cleared the awkwardness between them and would allow them to start afresh today.

As he pulled on his boots the image of Miss Carpenter's expression as they had paused outside her door came back to him. It had been no more than five seconds, but they had both lingered just a fraction longer than they should and in those few seconds something had passed between them.

'Impossible,' he murmured. He would not deny that objectively Miss Carpenter was an attractive young woman. She had deep brown eyes and full lips set in a pretty heart-shaped face. Her hair was a golden blonde and last night he'd seen it unpinned and cascading down her back. As he'd walked her back to her room he'd caught the faint hint of roses and he'd wondered if she used scented soap to wash the long locks.

Richard shook his head, trying to rid himself of the picture of Miss Carpenter in the bath lathering rose-scented soap into her hair.

This was not why he had returned and he needed no distractions, certainly not in the one woman his mother deemed irreplaceable when talking about looking after Lord Digby.

It was not wholly unexpected. He was only human and as likely to notice an attractive young woman as the next man, perhaps even more so. He had denied himself any intimacy in the years he had been away. It hadn't seemed right when Frederick Godrum, the man whose death he was responsible for, would never again get to kiss a woman, would never marry or settle down. The least Richard could do was deny himself the same.

No doubt it had been nothing more than tiredness last night and a lack of companionship. He could overcome that.

He was surprised to hear his father's voice in the main hall, deep and sonorous and sounding as if he were commanding the household once again. Richard stood quickly, not wanting there to be a repeat of the day before when his father escaped the watchful eyes that normally kept him safe and made his way to the river.

'Mr Digby, good morning,' Miss Carpenter said as Richard stepped out into the hall. She showed no awkwardness, no hint of what had passed between them the night before and for a moment Richard wondered if he had imagined it all.

'Good morning, Miss Carpenter.'

'Lord Digby and I were on our way to the glasshouse. There are some seedlings that need to be transferred to bigger pots. That is right, isn't it, Lord Digby?'

'Yes, lots to do this morning,' Lord Digby said, moving away.

Richard found it difficult every time his father looked through him, every time he failed to recognise his only son, but he tried not to show it.

'Perhaps I could lend a hand,' Richard said. He made the suggestion nonchalantly, trying not to let on how much it would mean to him to spend some proper time with his father.

'What a fantastic idea,' Miss Carpenter said. 'You always say the more hands the better, don't you, Lord Digby?'

'Yes, we have a lot to do,' Lord Digby said, leading the way through the house to the set of glass doors in the morning room that led out on to a beautiful terrace. The glasshouse was set at one end of the terrace, separate from the main building of the house with its own entrance.

'He seems well this morning,' Richard said as he fell into step beside Rose.

'He is happy this morning, although he did become a little unsettled when he was asking for your mother. I suggested he might like to work with his seedlings to distract him, but I do not know how long it will last.'

'Let us hope he will become engrossed in his work and forget about my mother for a while.'

They walked the rest of the way in silence, following Lord Digby into the humid building. Richard marvelled at the way his father went straight to the work bench without having to be guided. He had lost the ability to do so many things for himself, yet when he was faced with the familiar environment here in the glasshouse he was able to remember what needed to be done.

'I enjoy watching him work,' Miss Carpenter said as she took a seat opposite Lord Digby.

Richard followed her lead, marvelling at how relaxed she was. It was as though she didn't worry about any potential for harm, any accidents that might happen or dangerous outbursts—instead, she chatted away to Lord Digby, her voice soothing and trusting in equal measure. Richard saw how his father calmed at the sound of Miss Carpenter's voice and wondered if he would ever react to his son in that way.

'He struggles with remembering when things need repotting, but with gentle reminders he still can carry out the practical aspects of growing something from seed.'

Richard watched as his father inspected the seedlings and then selected a few bigger pots. Methodically, he filled them with soil and then ever so gently lifted the small plants from the pots they were in to their new, larger containers. He worked painfully slowly at times, but the end result was passable if not neat.

'Go and help him,' Miss Carpenter urged, leaning in and nudging him with her elbow. It was a familiar gesture, but he could not find it in himself to mind, quite enjoying the encouraging smile she gave him as he stood and walked round the work bench to his father.

'Shall I hold the pot steady?' he said quietly, feeling inordinately pleased when his father gave him an appraising look and then nodded, passing him the pot. 'What are you planting?'

'These will be poppies soon. My dear Penelope's favourite flower,' Lord Digby said without looking up. 'Every year I sow the seeds and every year I pick the first poppy and present it to my wife as a symbol of our love.'

'That is a wonderful thing to do,' Richard said, his voice catching in his throat. 'I am sure Lady Digby loves that tradition.'

They worked in silence for a while, Lord Digby filling the pots and transferring the seedlings while Richard held everything steady. It was a different kind of work to what he was used to, but as his father beamed up at him, placing the last seedling in its new container, he realised this was just as important as the work he had thrown himself into these last few years.

Part of his motivations for helping the small communities rebuild after natural disasters had struck had been selfish. There was always a vast amount of heavy manual labour involved, first in clearing the debris and then moving and transporting the materials that would be needed to rebuild the homes and public buildings of the towns and villages.

Each day he would work until he was so physically exhausted he could not do any more, not until he had rested his weary muscles for a while. Then he would collapse into bed, too tired to think about the guilt he was carrying. He also reasoned it was good penance.

One day he would stand before God and be judged for his deeds. Deep down he knew his place in heaven was far from guaranteed after he had been responsible for the death of another man, but it did not mean he had stopped caring about the people he encountered in the world. Slowly, he hoped that by going to those who truly needed his help, he was at least doing a little good while he had the chance.

'They need a little water every day,' Lord Digby said, smiling at Richard. 'I'll check on them, but it'll be your job to make sure they're watered and cared for. Mind you do not give them too much water, though, just a little every single day.'

'I will remember,' Richard said with a smile as his father clapped him on the shoulder.

'Right, now it is time for my morning ride. Tell the stableboy to ready the horses.'

Richard glanced at Miss Carpenter's and saw her eyes widen in panic.

'I wonder, Father, if you would like to come out in my phaeton. I haven't taken you for a ride for so long and I would like your opinion on how the horses are pulling.'

Lord Digby's face lit up and he began to move immediately.

'Splendid idea.'

Richard followed his father outside, feeling Miss Carpenter's hand on his arm. 'That was a good idea,' she said, smiling at him. 'I understand your father used to be a keen horseman, but he hasn't been able to ride in quite some time. I think it is one of the things he misses the most. He often asks us to ready his horse and it is heartbreaking to see his disappointment each time when we tell him he can no longer ride.'

'I will speak to the groom and check the phaeton is maintained, but hopefully we can take him for a ride around the lanes.'

'I will go and get a blanket for Lord Digby's knees and ensure he has everything he needs.'

Richard watched her go. He was surprised to find how much her approval meant to him and he felt a warmth inside him as he went to speak to the man in charge of the stables.

Fifteen minutes later they were squeezed on to the seat of the phaeton. Richard sat in the middle so he could hold the reins easily without having to lean, with his father on one side and Miss Carpenter on the other. It was a snug fit, but the look on his father's face as he urged the horses on was worth a few minutes of mild discomfort.

They trotted down the drive at a sedate pace, enjoying the late-morning sunshine. There was a slight breeze that brought the smells of early summer—honeysuckle and wild roses—and Richard realised how much he had missed England at this time of year. His travels had taken him all around the world, but nowhere could compare to this corner of Cambridgeshire.

For a moment he allowed himself to think of the future. He was aware his father might not survive another winter and that his health would fade over the next few months. When making his plans to return he had resolutely not allowed himself to think past his homecoming, not wanting to acknowledge there would be more difficult decisions ahead.

Some of the decisions about the future were out of his hands. When he had left England eight years ago he had been unsure if he would be pursued by the authorities, seeking justice for what he had done. With the benefit of hindsight and a little distance from the tragedy he could see he was unlikely to face the noose for his part in the death of Frederick Godrum.

However, he did not want to do anything that might add to the devastation Godrum's family would still be feeling at losing such a bright and energetic young man. If him being out of the country so they never had to worry about bumping into him while they were out and about made their lives a little better, Richard would leave.

He tried to put thoughts of the future from his mind. Right now he needed to concentrate on making his father's last months as comfortable as possible. He had neglected his family for far too long—now he had a lot to make up for.

Beside him he was aware of Miss Carpenter leaning forward, one hand holding the bonnet in place on her head, the other gripping the edge of the phaeton. Her expression was one of pure joy, and Richard felt drawn to her. It had been a long time since he had experienced any emotion other than guilt and sadness, and to see her made so happy from something as simple as a ride in a phaeton was striking.

'This is incredible,' Miss Carpenter said as she caught him looking at her.

'Have you never been in a phaeton before?'

She laughed. 'No, Mr Digby. Servants don't normally spend their time riding around in phaetons and curricles.'

'You've been in a carriage before?'

'I travelled by coach from London when I first came to St Ives, but that is the only time.'

'You didn't travel with the children you looked after in your last position?'

'There was never the need. The house was in the middle of the town so we walked everywhere local.'

'This phaeton is comfortable and safe, but for a truly thrilling ride you want to experience a curricle,' he said, thinking of the first time he had taken the reins in his friend's curricle. The small carriage had rocked and jolted with every bump in the road, but it had felt as though he were flying. Richard had resolved to buy a curricle one day, but that had been before the disaster that had led to him fleeing the country. Curricles and horses had been put far from his mind.

He checked on his father sitting beside him, but the old man was equally as thrilled with the phaeton ride, sitting comfortably on the bench seat and watching the world go by with a serene expression on his face.

Richard guided the horses through the narrow lanes of Hemingford Grey, following the road towards St Ives. It was quiet this way and they only encountered a few labourers who raised their hats as the phaeton passed, pausing for a moment from their work in the fields.

He slowed as they approached the bridge at St Ives with the horses walking sedately as they crossed over the river and made their way through the cobbled streets. His plan was to circle around Market Square and then retrace the route home before his father began to tire.

It was busy in St Ives with plenty of people making the most of the sunny day to linger as they went about their daily routines. The shops were bustling and people were standing and talking to friends and acquaintances. Richard circled around the square and made his way back over the bridge.

The road on the other side had been clear only a few minutes earlier when they had travelled in the opposite direction, but now there was a crowd of people blocking the way, craning their necks to get a view of what was happening. Richard stood on the footplate and looked over the crowd, catching a glimpse of two men circling each other and shouting in the middle of the assembled group of onlookers. They were young, only about eighteen or twenty, both well dressed in fine clothes.

There was no way through and no other way across the river, so Richard brought the phaeton to a halt, eyeing his father nervously. The old man had been contented throughout the trip out, but an encounter like this might make him agitated and that could be dangerous while he was in the phaeton.

'Can you hold the horses?' he said, passing the reins to Miss Carpenter.

She looked unsure, but nodded all the same, gripping the leather straps tightly in her hands. Richard jumped down, pausing for a moment by the two horses to stroke their noses and murmur some soothing words, then he gently shouldered his way to the front of the crowd to get an idea what was going on.

As he stepped to the front, he saw one young man take his glove and in an exaggerated show of anger and defiance fling it to the floor in front of the other man.

'I will have my satisfaction,' he said loudly. 'Tomorrow, at dawn.'

Richard felt the blood drain from his head and for a moment the ground seemed to tilt underneath his feet.

He was taken back eight years to the pivotal moment in his life, the moment all his troubles stemmed from. So many times he had willed himself back to that moment, wished he could have dealt with it differently. He wished he could have turned away and ignored the slight upon his honour, realised that there were far more important things in life than being called a cad and a scoundrel.

The man who had been challenged to a duel looked ready to punch the first, but managed to control his fury, instead nodding abruptly but not saying anything.

Neither of them was backing down. This challenge had been issued in public, reputations were on the line and for boys of eighteen there was nothing more important.

Richard looked at the crowd, stepping out into the circle that contained the two arguing men.

'Go about your business,' he called, his tone stern and brooking no argument. People here might not know him, but his clothes and manner marked him as someone with authority, someone who should be listened to. For a moment no one moved, but then slowly people started to trickle away. Richard wasn't sure if they were obeying his command or if they thought the best of the drama was over and finished, but right now he didn't care.

The two young men were still staring intently at one another, neither wanting to be the first to break away. When he was sure they didn't have too much of an audience, Richard approached, bending down to pick up the glove the first man had thrown at the feet of the second. It was a dramatic way to challenge someone to a duel, more at home in sensational serialisation in one of the newspapers than on the streets of St Ives.

'I believe this is yours,' Richard said, keeping his voice mild and calm.

'Move away, sir,' the first man said, taking his glove. 'You have no place here.'

'You are friends, are you not?' Richard said, looking between the men.

'We were,' the second man answered while the first just scoffed.

'Then do not make the foolish mistake of thinking *anything* is worth risking the life of another person, let alone someone you once called a friend.'

'This is none of your concern,' the first man said.

'It is entirely my concern,' Richard said, spinning to face him. 'Think this through for a moment. Think rationally, put aside the emotion and the anger and really think about the challenge you have issued. What will happen? You face each other tomorrow morning in a misty field, pistols pointed at one another?'

'It is a matter of honour,' the first man said.

'No,' Richard snapped. 'It is a matter of stupidity. Are you willing to shoot this man? To take his life? To be a murderer for ever?'

There was a flicker of uncertainty in the man's eye, so Richard pressed his advantage.

'Are you brave enough to sit across from his mother and explain why you have murdered her son?' Richard raised an eyebrow in question, but there was no answer. 'The alternative is that he shoots you. Dead. For ever. There is no coming back from that. Which is it that you would prefer?'

The man began to look a little uncomfortable.

'I asked you a question,' Richard said, raising his voice a little. 'Which do you prefer? To murder or to be killed?'

'It is not murder. It is a matter of honour.'

'No. It is murder. Nothing less. If you point a pistol at another and they die, that is murder. You will have to live with the consequences for the rest of your life.'

The first man began shifting from foot to foot and Richard could see he was starting to doubt his actions.

'Whatever wrong has been done, perceived or real, there is another way. Forget about the duel and solve this another way.'

'There is no other honourable way,' the second man said.

'Of course there is,' Richard said, turning to the second man. 'Challenge him to a boxing match and get in a few good punches if you feel the need to be violent, or act like the men you are trying to be and solve this with words.'

He levelled a long, hard stare at both young men and then spun and walked away. It was impossible to know if they would heed his words or if they would continue with their plan to duel, but at the very least he had made them think about the impact of their actions.

His hands were shaking as he climbed back into the phaeton, ignoring Miss Carpenter's concerned look. With a flick of the reins, the horses began moving, trotting past the two young men who watched the phaeton go silently.

Once they were out of the town, travelling through the lanes leading to Hemingford Grey, Miss Carpenter leaned into him, her body brushing against his in the confines of the small carriage.

'That was a good thing you did,' she murmured in his ear. She didn't press him, didn't enquire why he was quite so vocal about the arguments of two men he did not know. Instead, she gave him an encouraging smile and then turned her attention back to his father.

Chapter Nine

Rose stood in the shadows watching Mr Digby as he raised the axe and brought it down on the wood, cracking the log in half. His expression was fixed into a frown and there was a faint sheen of perspiration on his brow as he hefted the axe again. He had been going at the wood for at least ten minutes and showed no sign of stopping.

It was a curious feature of his personality, this need to be occupied much of the time. She had observed him when he sat still and there was this energy about him, ebbing and flowing, as if it took a lot of effort not to jump up and start doing some physical task.

After a final moment of hesitation, she stepped from the shadows and out into the sunshine, waiting for Mr Digby to notice her arrival.

'Good afternoon, Miss Carpenter,' he said, not taking his eyes off the wood in front of him, swinging the axe again and making the log splinter.

'Good afternoon, Mr Digby.'

'How is my father?'

'Resting. He often has a lie down after lunch and

will sleep for a few hours. Mr Watkins is sitting with him while I stretch my legs.' She paused, watching as he threw the splinters of wood into a basket and selected another log to begin chopping up. 'I wanted to check on you after the encounter in St Ives earlier.'

She saw his eyes widen in surprise. Rose had never struggled with saying what she was thinking. It was a trait that had got her into trouble on many occasions when she was younger. Now she could control her tongue a little better, but she did not see the point of skirting round a subject, talking in an abstract fashion when things were a lot clearer if you just came out and said what you meant.

'Thank you, Miss Carpenter,' he said, his expression turning serious. 'I am quite well.'

'Did you know those young men?'

'No.'

'Not many people would have stepped in like that, not when it was a matter between strangers.'

Mr Digby regarded her for a long moment and Rose wondered if he would dismiss her. There was a good chance he did not wish to talk about whatever it was that had prompted his impassioned speech about the damage a duel could cause, but she was curious enough to ask anyway.

'I think I am done here,' he said, looking at the impressive pile of wood he had chopped, heaped in the basket. 'Would you care for a stroll by the river? I feel the need for some gentle exercise.'

'That would be lovely, Mr Digby.'

He had shed his jacket and waistcoat at some point while wielding the axe and had rolled his shirtsleeves up to his elbow. Now he made no move to put on his discarded layers, instead disappearing inside with the jacket and waistcoat to deposit them.

They walked in silence around the side of the house and into the planted area of the garden. Beyond that a wide lawn stretched down towards the river. There was a path that wound along the banks, taking a route through the grounds of Meadow View and then out to the fields beyond. Rose had walked a few miles of it, ending up in the next pretty little village of Hemingford Abbots.

The path was a little overgrown this time of year, with long grass leaning in and early summer flowers adding little bursts of colour. Bees weaved their way from flower to flower and in the trees the birds chirped and sang. It was an idyllic scene, one that was ideal for discussing a sensitive topic.

For a while they did not say anything. Only when the path widened and they could walk side by side did Mr Digby begin to speak.

'I am sure that you have heard the rumours about why I left England eight years ago, Miss Carpenter.'

'I try not to listen to rumours, Mr Digby,' Rose said, looking across at him. He looked troubled and she hoped she wasn't adding to his worries, pressing him like this. 'I know there was some trouble and you had to leave the country, but no more.'

He gave a wry smile that did not reach his eyes. 'We always think people are talking about us whereas often they are much too involved in their own lives, preoccupied with their own troubles, to think of what anyone else is doing.' He shook his head and then continued.

'Eight years ago I made a stupid decision. I let my anger and my pride get the better of me and because of my actions a man died.'

'That's terrible. What happened?'

Mr Digby cleared his throat and uprooted a long piece of grass, pulling it apart as he spoke.

'I was out with my friends, a group of carefree young men who had nothing more to worry about than how much we had lost at cards earlier in the evening. Everyone had imbibed a little too much and someone suggested we attend one of the dances at the Assembly Rooms. We were too drunk for it, but we were the sons of the wealthiest landowners in the area so they allowed us to enter.'

His eyes were fixed on a point in the distance and Rose wondered if it was cathartic for him to finally tell his story. She had the sense he didn't often talk about what had happened all those years ago. 'We drank some more, danced a little, and then I spotted Amelia Godrum. She was a young woman of nineteen, the sister of a man who lived close by, someone I had grown up with. I approached her and asked her to dance, even though by this time my footwork was sloppy and my words slurred.'

Rose found it hard to imagine Mr Digby losing control of himself, but she supposed eight years and a horrific tragedy would change a man.

'We danced, but Frederick Godrum, Amelia's brother, thought I held her too tightly. He was furious and followed me out of the Assembly Rooms. He called me a cad and a scoundrel and insisted I make things right with Amelia.' Mr Digby shook his head and pulled another long piece of grass from the bank, starting to shred it. 'I laughed and told him he was being ridiculous. I respected Amelia, but I was not going to marry her. There must have been something condescending in my tone for he became enraged and challenged me to a duel, saying I was without honour.'

Rose nodded slowly, realising why Mr Digby had been so impassioned when he had seen the two foolish young men contemplating a duel on the bridge in St Ives earlier.

'What happened?'

'I sobered up. I thought Frederick's temper would have cooled, too, and when I set out for the spot chosen for the duel I never thought he would want to go through with it. We were friends, not especially close, but two men from similar worlds. I thought in the cold light of day he would accept my apology.'

'But he didn't?'

'No. He was still furious and demanded I marry his sister. I laughed and told him he was being unreasonable.' Mr Digby shook his head and threw the last piece of grass away with a flick of his hand. Rose could see every muscle in his body was tense as if his body wanted to flee rather than remember.

'You faced him in a duel?'

'I refused at first, but he called me a coward. I was twenty-two years old and back then I thought being a called a coward was the worst thing that could happen to a man, so I picked up a pistol.'

Rose wondered if he had shot his friend, hardly able to believe this measured, cool man next to her was capable of such an act of violence.

'We paced and turned to face each other. Even then I thought he would shoot in the air. He would have made his point and honour would have been satisfied.'

Rose didn't pretend to understand the intricacies of the rules of duels. They were a ridiculous way to settle a dispute and illegal for good reason.

'He pointed the pistol at me, but I still believed he would shoot up. I raised my pistol, too, and I fired it once into the air.'

'You didn't shoot him?'

'No. I would never have shot him.'

'But he died?'

'He pulled the trigger and his pistol misfired...'

Mr Digby swallowed and Rose saw the emotion in his eyes as he pressed on.

'He turned the pistol round, to look down the barrel to see what had happened, and at that moment the shot was released.'

'He shot himself?'

'At close range, in the face.'

For a long moment Rose was quiet as she tried to take in everything Mr Digby had told her.

'So, you see why I could not stand by when those foolish young men were posturing over some supposed insult and risking their lives to satisfy their honour. There is nothing worse than being responsible for the death of another man.'

'You didn't kill Mr Godrum,' Rose said quietly.

'I didn't shoot him,' Mr Digby corrected her quietly, 'but I am responsible for his death.'

She didn't feel able to argue with him although she wasn't sure she agreed. For eight years this tragic event had eaten into his conscience, festering like a deep wound.

'There were witnesses?'

'Yes, his second and mine, and a doctor, as is proper.'

'Yet you still had to leave the country?'

'I may not have pulled the trigger on the pistol that killed Frederick, but duelling itself is illegal. His family were understandably devastated and his father made it known if I ever set foot in England again he would do everything in his power to ensure I was prosecuted.'

'It is hard to reason with a grief-stricken man,' Rose murmured.

'Indeed. So, I stayed away. It was the right thing to do. None of Frederick's family should have to go through the discomfort of spotting me on the street, of seeing me getting on with my life when Frederick is dead.'

'You carry a lot of guilt with you, Mr Digby,' Rose said, knowing she was overstepping. Although Mr Digby had felt it appropriate to confide in her after his actions on the bridge in St Ives, it didn't mean he wanted her opinion on the choices he had made these last few years.

'It is not misplaced, Miss Carpenter. I know what you are trying to say—over the years people have gently tried to tell me that it was not my fault. I did not challenge Frederick Godrum to a duel, I did not shoot him, I did not turn that pistol and make him look down the barrel. I know I did not do any of that, but his death would not have happened if it weren't for me. If I had reacted differently, if I had not let my own pride get in the way of good sense, a young man would not have died. I *have* to take responsibility for that.'

Mr Digby had stopped walking and turned to face her, and Rose saw the anguish he was carrying manifest itself in his expression. Logic might tell Mr Digby he was not a murderer, but that did not stop him feeling like one.

Instinctively, she reached out and took his hand, looking down at her fingers entwined with his. It was inappropriate and uninvited, but Mr Digby did not pull away. Instead, he looked at her intently as if searching for something he had lost.

'I have no right to tell you what to feel,' Rose said quietly. 'But I do understand why you were quite so vocal with those young men today. It must be difficult to see people about to make the same mistakes that ruined your life.'

'Yes.' He looked as though he wanted to say more, but the words wouldn't come.

Rose felt a flood of compassion for this man. She had thought him distant and cool, sometimes even aloof. She had disliked him for the years he had spent away from his loving family, thinking him selfish not to realise what a wonderful thing it was to have parents who cared for you. Now she could see the pain he had suffered and the weight of the guilt he carried these past eight years and she could understand a little his need to stay away.

Here in Hemingford Grey, he was the son of a baron, one day due to inherit a profitable estate and a beautiful house. Life would follow a predictable but comfortable path—marriage, children and building the family wealth to pass down to the next generation. If he had stayed, every day he would be living a life Frederick

Godrum would never get to experience. At least if he went elsewhere, spent his time in less hospitable parts of the world, it was punishment as well as penance for his actions.

'Thank you for confiding in me,' Rose said softly, unable to tear her gaze away from his. He had pale blue eyes that drew you in and she felt an inexplicable connection to him in that moment. His thumb grazed over the back of her hand, caressing the skin ever so gently, and Rose's body swayed towards him.

There was a rustle in the undergrowth and Rose took a hurried step back as a dog appeared, shattering the moment. She felt momentarily stunned, confused at what had just passed between them. Quickly, she turned, knowing she would not be able to control the expression on her face and not wanting Mr Digby to see how much he had affected her.

'Digby, it is you,' a jovial voice called out as a man appeared around the bend in the path.

Mr Digby glanced at Rose and then seemed to compose himself, smiling at the approaching man and then crouching down to stroke the terrier that was impatiently jumping at his legs.

Chapter Ten

Richard used the distraction of the yapping white terrier to cover his confusion. It had been difficult explaining about the duel and the foolish decisions that had changed the course of his life to Miss Carpenter, but it had felt like the right thing to do after she had witnessed his impassioned speech to the young men in St Ives. He didn't owe Miss Carpenter any sort of explanation, but he realised he was beginning to trust and respect the young woman who was such a big part of both his parents' lives.

In a way it had felt freeing to tell Miss Carpenter some of the story that he had kept so close for so long. Then she had reached out for his hand, a gesture of comfort and solidarity, yet he had felt a flicker of something more just like the night before when he had walked her back to her room.

He didn't want to have to think about it. Miss Carpenter was being friendly and supportive, nothing more, and even if she was, he had no right to seek a connection with her.

'Sebastian,' Richard said as his old friend came closer and called the dog to heel. 'I didn't know you were in the country.'

Lord Cambridgeshire took his responsibilities seriously and during the winter months spent his time in London so he could attend Parliament. It was late May now and often Parliament would be sitting at this time of year.

'I returned home last week. Elizabeth is unwell.'

'I am so sorry.'

'She rallies. It is congestion in the lungs, but we are hopeful she will recover.'

Lord Cambridgeshire had six children and Elizabeth was the eldest from what Richard could recall from the letters his friend had sent him at regular intervals.

'It is good to see you,' Sebastian said, clapping Richard on the back.

'Thank you for your last letter.'

'It prompted you to return home?'

'Yes. My mother wrote every week, but not once did she mention my father's condition.'

'It is the role of mothers everywhere to protect their children,' Sebastian said. 'I am glad you decided to come. It must be a relief for Lady Digby to have you home.'

'I think so. She was exhausted and has gone to stay with her sister for a week to recuperate.'

'You must be pleased, Miss Carpenter,' Sebastian said, turning to the young woman who up until now had been standing silently a little distance away. Richard was thrown for a moment, surprised that they knew each other.

'I am, my lord,' Miss Carpenter said, smiling warmly at Sebastian. 'My lady is so dedicated to Lord Digby, but I have care for her health as well.'

Sebastian must have seen the confusion on Richard's face for he threw his head back and laughed. 'Digby is wondering how we know one another, Miss Carpenter.'

'Lord Cambridgeshire calls on Lady Digby every week without fail when he is in the country and sends a very generous basket every week when he is in London,' Miss Carpenter said.

'You always were the best of men, Sebastian.'

'Don't get sentimental on me, Digby. I am just pleased you're home. You look well. Tired, but well. I suppose it was a long way to travel.'

'It is so good to see you.'

'You must come over and meet the family. The children are all eager to see the man they have heard so much about.'

'And I am keen to see them…' Richard hesitated '…but will Lady Cambridgeshire mind?'

Sebastian shook his head. 'No, she will want to see you, too. I have read her your letters over the years and she has much love in her heart for you. She knows the truth of what happened and has no malice towards you.'

'Then I will gladly come.'

'Good, that is settled. Perhaps tomorrow afternoon. Amelia is talking of a picnic in the garden of Houghton Hall. Bring your father if you think he would enjoy it. Now I had better get back to Elizabeth. This troublesome creature is her dog and I promised to take him for a walk, but she will fret if I do not have him back soon. Come, Nibbles, let us go see Elizabeth.'

'Give her my best wishes,' Richard said, watching as Sebastian bowed to Miss Carpenter and turned to walk away, calling the little dog to heel.

They stood watching him go for a moment, then Miss Carpenter raised an eyebrow.

'Amelia?'

'Amelia, Countess of Cambridgeshire,' he said grimly.

'Born Amelia Godrum?'

'Yes. It complicates matters somewhat.'

'She married your closest friend.'

'She did. They were secretly betrothed when Frederick challenged me to the duel—it made the whole thing even more ridiculous. Amelia had always been in love with Sebastian and he with her, there was no doubt they would marry, but a grander match was expected for Sebastian and they needed a few more months of secrecy.'

'You have not seen her since her brother's death?'

'Only once. After Frederick died, I went to his house and asked to see his parents. Amelia was there then, trying to keep the peace as always.'

'It does not sound as if she holds any grudge against you.'

'No, I expect not. She is too good, too sweet, to have malicious thoughts.' If she wanted to see him, then he would, of course, but the last thing he wanted was to dredge up painful memories for the young woman. 'I did not know you were acquainted with Lord Cambridgeshire.'

'He had been very good to your mother these past couple of years,' Miss Carpenter said, 'And he is a true gentleman.'

Richard frowned, not understanding her meaning. Miss Carpenter laughed at his expression, the sound lifting him from the melancholy that had settled about him.

'Of course he is a gentleman, he is an earl.'

'I mean a gentleman in his behaviour. So many who are classed as gentlemen behave superior, looking down on those in the classes below them. They bark orders and take advantage of their superior position. Lord Cambridgeshire knows he is in a social class well above my own, but he would never seek to emphasise the fact.'

'You are right, of course, he is a considerate man…' Richard paused, regarding her curiously. 'You have had experience of a so-called gentleman treating you poorly.'

Miss Carpenter hesitated, her eyes sliding away from his. 'Yes,' she said and then abruptly turned away, starting back towards home. He considered pressing the matter—he had confided so much in her—but was aware that, for someone who normally said what she was thinking to shy away from a conversation, it must be a painful topic, so instead he followed her in silence.

As they reached the point where the path entered the garden of Meadow View, Miss Carpenter turned and looked over her shoulder at him.

'You should go to the picnic,' she said decisively.

Richard had to suppress a smile. Most housemaids or companions would not dare to have an opinion on their master's social life, but Miss Carpenter let her opinion be known on everything. It was refreshing to have an exchange like this, for someone to tell him exactly what they thought—it reminded him of when he had been away.

Then it hadn't mattered he was the son of a baron, one day to inherit a fortune and a title. Things had been different on the journey home. His name and wealth had meant he could travel quickly and in style, but people had treated him differently. There was more distance, more formality.

'Lord Cambridgeshire invited my father as well. Do you think he will be well enough to attend?'

'It depends on the day, although, after seeing how happy he was going out in the phaeton today, perhaps he could attend for a short while.' She thought for a moment. 'If he is well, we could take the carriage, ensure Mr Watkins comes, too, and perhaps stay a short while. Then Mr Watkins and I could take Lord Digby home while you stay and enjoy your friend's company.' She bit her lip, and Richard found his gaze drawn to her mouth. Her lips were full and rosy and he had the sudden urge to lean forward and brush a kiss against them. The thought surprised him and he jerked back even though they were not standing that close. Thankfully, Miss Carpenter was distracted enough not to notice.

'Although sometimes going anywhere out of the familiar does unsettle him.'

'Let us wait and see,' Richard said, trying to look anywhere but her lips. 'Whatever is best for him on the day.'

They paused as they reached the bottom of the lawn where they would have to turn and head back to the house.

'Thank you for the stroll and for confiding in me,'

Miss Carpenter said, raising her eyes to meet his for a second. Something sparked and fizzed between them and then quickly she turned and began hurrying towards the house.

Rose closed the kitchen door behind her and rested her head on the wood for a moment.

'Something amiss, dear?' Mrs Green said as she bustled into the room from the pantry.

'No, I am a little overcome with the heat, that is all. It is a glorious day out there.' Rose spoke quickly, not wanting the astute older woman to think there was anything else going on.

'There's some cold lemonade in the pantry, I made it for when Lord Digby wakes up. I thought if he is going out in the glasshouse this afternoon, he will need something to keep him cool. Let me get you a glass.'

Rose began to protest, but Mrs Green waved a dismissive hand and fetched her a glass, pressing her on to one of the stools around the large kitchen table.

'You still have another half an hour until Lord Digby normally wakes. There is no rush, Rose.'

Rose sank into the seat and sipped the refreshing drink. It was delicious, like all of Mrs Green's creations, and she allowed herself to savour it. The cook continued to work around her, bringing vegetables from the pantry to start preparing for the evening meal.

As she drank, Rose mulled over everything Mr Digby had told her while they were walking by the river. It made so much sense, explained so many things. It was a tragedy, an awful accident, and she didn't think he was right to shoulder all the responsibility for his friend's death, but she could understand why he felt that way.

She wondered if there was any chance of lessening his guilt, of showing him that he might have made mistakes in his youth, but that did not mean he did not deserve to have a normal life now, a happy life. She thought of Lady Digby, the woman who had been so kind to her, and the cloud of melancholy the woman lived under.

Mr Digby was here at the moment to fulfil his duty, to aid while his father slipped further into the madness of old age that was consuming him, but what would happen when Lord Digby passed away? Mr Digby would leave, would seek out once again dangerous parts of the world to lose himself in to try to make up for the wrong he thought he had done. It would break Lady Digby's heart.

'You look pensive,' Mrs Green said as she selected a carrot and started chopping.

'I was thinking of Lady Digby,' Rose said quickly. 'I hope she is resting and recovering her strength.'

'She will need it,' Mrs Green said grimly.

'Yes, the next few months are not going to be easy.'

'At least Mr Digby is home now.'

Rose nodded. 'Do you think he will stay?'

Mrs Green looked at her curiously and then shrugged. 'I expect for a while. Once Lord Digby passes, he will inherit the title, but I doubt he will want to take up his place here.'

'It is a shame,' Rose said quietly, 'that he is denying himself the life he should have had.' She saw Mrs

Green's intrigued expression and pushed on quickly. 'Lady Digby will be devastated when he leaves again.'

'She will,' Mrs Green said. 'But she'll still have you. Unless you're hiding a young man you're sweet on somewhere.'

Rose scoffed and shook her head.

'Don't laugh, dear, you're young and pretty and one day some young man will catch your eye.'

She was still young and one day she did want to marry. After her affair with Mr Rampton she had thought she would never want to go near another man again, but over the months she had realised the only person she was hurting with that vow was herself. Instead, she had resolved to one day find herself a nice man, someone who was her equal, who would listen to her opinions and treat her as a partner in life, not an inferior.

Rose drained the glass and stood, eager to get out of the kitchen before she let slip something she did not mean to. She was hit by the memory of how Mr Digby had looked at her, the fizz of attraction passing between them as they stood on the banks of the river.

'Foolish girl,' she murmured to herself as she left the room. The last thing she needed was any complication of the heart in this position. She was happy here, happy with her work and happy working for Lady Digby.

She had been a mess when she had arrived in St Ives, but Lady Digby had scooped her up and helped her rebuild her shattered confidence. Not for one moment did she think Mr Digby was anything like her previous employer, but she was older now, wiser in the ways of the world, and she had first hand experience that any relationship between a man of Mr Digby's social status and a housemaid could not end well.

Chapter Eleven

Rose tried to keep calm, pacing backwards and forwards in time with the distressed old man. He had woken disorientated and grouchy, but as the afternoon had worn on the disorientation had turned to agitation and she was fast running out of ideas on how to keep him safe and settled.

'Come, Lord Digby, sit for a moment and I will read to you,' she said, reaching out for his hand. He shook her off and shrank away, not seeming to recognise her. It was not unusual for him to forget who she was. He never remembered her name, but after two years sometimes there was a flash of recognition. Today, though, there was nothing.

'Leave me alone,' he muttered, lashing out with an arm.

'What do we do, Miss Carpenter?' Mr Watkins said from his position by the door. He was standing to attention, trying to adopt the pose of a conscientious valet ready to spring to his master's aid, but in truth his aim was to guard the door.

Rose desperately trawled through her mind for what had worked in the past. Already this afternoon she had tried to take him to his plants in the glasshouse and had read to him from his favourite book, but neither of these things had helped. Normally, her words could soothe him, but today nothing was getting through.

'Music,' she declared. 'Do you play, Mr Watkins?' She motioned at the pianoforte in the corner of the room. Lady Digby played beautifully, often singing to accompany the relaxing melodies. Lord Digby could sit for hours listening to her.

'No.'

Rose bit her lip. She doubted any of the servants could play the piano—it wasn't something that was high on the list of priorities for education for people who were going to spend their life in service.

'I shall ask Mr Digby—perhaps he can play. I will be a few minutes…call if you need help.'

Quickly, she slipped from the room and headed for the study downstairs. The door was open and she saw Mr Digby behind the desk, a pile of papers in front of him. He smiled at her as she entered, but Rose could not summon anything cheerful in return.

'Can you play the piano?' she asked without any pre-amble.

'Yes. What has happened?'

'Your father is agitated. I have tried everything I would normally do, but he will not settle.'

Mr Digby frowned, but stood immediately, coming from behind the desk. 'The piano normally helps?'

'Lady Digby will often play to soothe Lord Digby if he becomes worked up. I do not have any other ideas.'

'Then we shall try this.'

Rose was grateful to find that Mr Digby came without protest or criticism—he seemed to be beginning to trust her judgement when it came to his father.

Upstairs, she knocked on the door softly and Mr Watkins opened it immediately. Lord Digby had not stopped pacing and did not pause even now. His head was bowed, his steps slow as he shuffled backwards and forwards across the carpet. Every so often he would mumble under his breath, but his words were not directed at anyone.

'Good afternoon, Father,' Mr Digby said, but he had the sense not to approach the agitated man. 'I thought I might play a little on the pianoforte, if you have no objections.'

He took a seat on the piano stool and then beckoned Rose over.

'What does he like?'

Rose shrugged. She had no musical knowledge whatsoever. Her early years had been spent traipsing from hovel to hovel or trying to survive on the street and, until her guardians had taken her in at the age of ten, she had not been able to read or write. Desperate not to be doomed to a life of poverty, Rose had worked hard at her lessons until she surpassed her peers in reading, writing and arithmetic, but there had been no space for anything more in her education.

'He likes the slow ones,' she said. 'They calm him.'

Mr Digby flexed his fingers and began to play. She was surprised that he didn't have to leaf through the sheets of music that were stacked on the music stand atop the piano or rifle through the papers hidden inside in the piano stool. Instead, he played from memory, his fingers dancing over the keys confidently.

At first the music seemed to have no effect on Lord Digby, but after a minute he stopped pacing and came to stand beside his son, watching him as the notes rang out. There was still a deep frown on the old man's face, still a look of fear and uncertainty, but it was not as intense as before and some of the agitation had melted away.

The first piece of music lasted only a couple of minutes, but Rose was pleased to see Lord Digby did not move away as the last note faded to silence.

'Have you any requests?' Mr Digby asked, looking up at his father.

The old man didn't answer so Mr Digby hovered his fingers over the keys again before selecting a piece himself.

Rose recognised this one as well and was relieved to see Lord Digby relax further as the familiar music washed over him. He stood, not moving, by his son's elbow, mesmerised by how Mr Digby's fingers travelled over the keys. Slowly, the music did its work and the frown on the old man's face lifted and was replaced by an expression of serenity.

They were on the fourth piece of music when Lord Digby suddenly moved from his position and approached Rose.

'May I have this dance?'

Rose blinked, uncertain. She knew Lord Digby liked to dance—sometimes Lady Digby would place her hand in his and they would sway together in time to some imagined music. Rose would do most things for Lord

Digby, but she didn't want to upset him by not knowing the steps he wanted her to take.

Hesitantly, she glanced at Mr Digby, who nodded in encouragement. Until a few years ago Rose had never danced before. It was another thing people of her background grew up not learning how to do. She shuddered when she thought of the last time a man had held out his hand in that expectant way and tried to push all thoughts of Mr Rampton, her previous employer, from her mind. The circumstances were very different and Lord Digby was an innocent.

She placed her hand in Lord Digby's, and he gently looped an arm around her back. His touch was feather-light, but he took the lead, guiding her round the room. Rose tried to smile, tried to relax, but it was too difficult to separate what was happening here from the traumatic memories of being forced into dancing with Mr Rampton.

Something must have shown on her face for Mr Digby stumbled over a few notes for the first time and as they passed the piano he leaned out and murmured quietly, 'Is something amiss?'

She gave him a tight smile, but did not answer, thankful for the moment the song came to an end and she could step away from Lord Digby.

'Thank you for the dance, my lord,' she said, trying to cover her discomfort with a light tone.

'I am tired. I would like to sit,' Lord Digby said and Rose felt the relief blossom inside her as he made his way to his favourite chair overlooking the garden and the river beyond.

Mr Digby played a few more gentle pieces quietly

in the background while Rose and Mr Watkins made Lord Digby comfortable, plumping the cushion he always sat with behind his back and fetching a tray of tea.

'Might I have a moment, Miss Carpenter?' Mr Digby said when Lord Digby was settled and happily staring out of the window at the view.

'Of course. Let me know if you need something, Mr Watkins.'

The valet nodded in response, taking a seat next to Lord Digby and speaking in a low voice to his master. Over the last couple of years, they had found that a gentle companionship was one of the best ways to keep Lord Digby calm and settled. At any time either Rose, Mr Watkins or Lady Digby would ensure they were present, close by, making observations about the view or the occurrences of the day. It seemed to keep Lord Digby grounded.

When Rose had first joined Lady Digby's household the Baroness had explained she did not expect Rose to work as the other maids. She might change Lord Digby's sheets or do some light tidying in Lord Digby's rooms, but her focus was the Baron.

Much of the time she would just need to be present, close by, a reassuring, friendly face to keep Lord Digby calm and happy. It was an unusual set up, but it worked, and between Rose and Mr Watkins they were able to foster an environment of peace and tranquillity as well as keep Lord Digby well-groomed and generally content.

Rose followed Mr Digby from the room, making sure the door clicked closed behind her before following him downstairs. He led her into the study and motioned for her to sit in one of the comfortable chairs. The study had once been Lord Digby's, but he hadn't set foot in it for a long time now.

Lady Digby took care of the essential estate business from her little writing desk in the drawing room and for a couple of years this room had been rarely entered. In the time he had been home Mr Digby had taken to setting himself up in the study in the evenings or sometimes mid-morning and Rose could see he was slowly making his way through the pile of paperwork Lady Digby had not had the time or inclination to deal with this past year.

'Thank you for playing the piano for Lord Digby,' Rose said as she perched on the edge of the chair. Although Lady Digby was kind to her and upstairs in Lord Digby's rooms Rose would sit back as she talked to the Baron, she felt a little uncomfortable relaxing in the study as if she were a guest.

'It was a good idea, Miss Carpenter. He calmed almost immediately.' Mr Digby smiled softly. 'My mother taught me to play when I was young and then I had a music tutor before I left for school. Sometimes during my lessons, I would catch a glimpse of my father, standing somewhere out of the way, trying to be unobtrusive, just listening to me play.'

'Lady Digby always reminds us that Lord Digby is the same person he always was. He has the same likes and dislikes, the same passions, it is just part of his mind that is failing. It does not mean he has changed completely.'

'She is right, of course. A man who has always liked listening to the piano and dancing is not suddenly going to hate it after sixty-five years, no matter what else is happening with him.' He looked at her seriously. 'You seemed uncomfortable in there, when my father asked you to dance.'

A shudder passed through Rose's body, and although she tried hard to conceal it, she could see Mr Digby noticed.

He cleared his throat and then leaned forward in his chair. He was sitting across from her, the two comfortable armchairs set at an angle to allow two people to talk, but also enjoy the views over the formal garden. Now his knees were almost touching hers.

'Has something happened before?' Mr Digby asked, his eyes coming up to meet hers. She thought of Mr Rampton, of all the months she had spent trying to reject his advances and the awful sense of disgust when she had finally given in.

Rose didn't know how to put anything into words so she sat there, completely still.

Mr Digby cleared his throat. 'Has my father been inappropriate towards you?'

'Lord Digby?' Rose said, then shook her head vigorously. 'Never, not once.'

The look of relief on Mr Digby's face was complete and all-consuming. He allowed his head to drop for a moment before he lifted it again, frowning.

'But you were uncomfortable.'

'Yes, but not because of your father. He has never once been inappropriate; despite his failing memory, he still only has eyes for your mother.'

'Someone else then? Someone here?'

Rose shook her head. 'No, do not for one moment think there is anyone in this house like that. Your mother would not allow it. She prides herself on having built a welcoming, loving family home where everyone feels safe and respected.' She swallowed hard and looked down at her hands. 'My last position was not in such a supportive environment.'

Mr Digby frowned, but motioned for her to go on.

'I was nanny to a young boy and girl. They were sweet enough children and I enjoyed the work. Their father was a widower and, at first, I barely saw him. He spent a lot of time in London seeing to business, but after a few months he returned home for a while.' Rose couldn't look up, couldn't tear her eyes away from her fingers that were bunched in the material of her dress.

'What happened?'

'He pursued me,' she said, making it sound much simpler than it had actually been. Every day she would be caught in this unpleasant game of cat and mouse. He stalked her through the halls of Thetford House, surprising her in dark corners where she least expected it. It had made every day a chore to get through and she had resolved to resign her position so many times. 'I resisted, but I think he just saw that as a challenge.'

'He wanted you to be his mistress?'

Rose hesitated. She never normally shared anything too personal, knowing it could make her vulnerable. Many people would hear the story of her liaison with her old master and label her as a harlot. In some places it might end up costing her a position alongside her reputation. She didn't think Mr Digby was like that and she thought back to earlier in the day when he had opened up to her and told her about his past when he did not owe her any sort of explanation.

'At first I think he just liked the idea of a quick fumble whenever it suited him, but as I rejected him, he became more and more obsessed with the idea of possessing me.' She glanced up and saw the suppressed anger in Mr Digby's eyes.

'For a long time I held out, but then one evening I received a letter informing me Sarah, the woman who had looked after me in childhood, had died suddenly. I was devastated and Mr Rampton saw that.'

'He took advantage of you.'

'He took advantage of my despair. Once again, I felt all alone in the world and he offered me comfort.' She felt a wave of nausea rise inside her as she remembered the way he had held her down, not stopping even as she sobbed into the pillow. It was not comfort he had resolved to give her in the end, instead catching her at her weakest moment and taking what he wanted, leaving her feeling worse than ever.

'I thought after that he would dismiss me, send me on my way. Or perhaps we would return to our normal positions—a good nanny is hard to find, after all—but he told me I was his mistress and I had no choice in the matter.'

'You didn't leave?'

Rose shook her head. 'Not at first. He had this persuasive way about him and could convince me he cared about me. In the darkness of the night, he would tell me we would be together, that he would marry me, then in the cold light of day he would treat me with contempt.'

'The worst sort of man.'

'He was, but very clever. He reeled me in by playing on my guilt and the loss of my virtue and then he kept me exactly where he wanted me by pushing me away and pulling me back to him.' She shivered and risked a look at Mr Digby. His opinion mattered to her, she realised with a jolt. She did not want him to think her a woman without morals, or a foolish girl who could be taken in by any man.

'Every evening he would order me to his study and then he would ask me to dance. I think he knew how uncomfortable it made me. I had never danced before and I was completely at his mercy. I hated the feeling of having to surrender my trust to him and I think he knew it.'

'That is what you felt when my father asked you to dance.'

'Yes. Even though I know your father is a kind man, a gentle man, it brought back the memories.'

'I am sorry, Miss Carpenter,' he said with a sad shake of his head. 'I cannot imagine what it must have been like living with a man like that and I am sorry you were reminded of it this afternoon.'

'Your mother calls me Rose, Mr Digby. Everyone except you calls me Rose.'

'You would like me to use your given name?'

'If you do not think it inappropriate.'

'Of course,' he said with a faint smile. He paused for a moment, looking at her with his intense blue eyes. 'How did you get away from him, Rose?'

'Mr Rampton? I was numb with grief for a while, from losing the first person who had ever loved me unconditionally. I mourned Sarah for months, but slowly I recovered from the shock and realised I was not living the life she would have wanted me to have.

'We were not wealthy by any stretch, but when I came to her and her husband, this filthy little street urchin, she resolved to use any money they had to ensure I had a good education. She wanted more for me than a life in the gutters, yet I was so unhappy I knew this wasn't what she had planned.' Rose paused and smiled faintly. 'Her love saved me. I packed my bags and confronted Mr Rampton. I refused to listen to any of his manipulative lies and then I left.'

'Is that when you came here?'

'Yes, I took the first coach I could find and it took me to Cambridge. While I was there I met your mother and father.'

'That led to you having a job here?'

Rose smiled at the memory, allowing her thoughts to turn away from the distasteful to a happier time.

'I was planning on returning to London. I had no family left, but I did have a few friends. I thought I might talk to one of those agencies that places nannies with families who are looking for someone, but I had to lodge overnight in Cambridge before the next coach to London.'

'It was a chance meeting, then?'

Rose nodded. 'Your mother had taken your father to visit one of the eminent doctors in Cambridge to see if there was anything that could be done. Lord Digby's memory issues were starting to become more obvious and I believe there had been a few uncomfortable incidents in public. The doctor had told your mother there was nothing to be done, but to be prepared for the future.'

She watched as Mr Digby grimaced and realised the

weight of the guilt he carried for this as well. He could never change the past few years, never alter the fact that he had not been there when his parents had most needed him, as they had come to terms with his father's illness.

'Lord Digby was understandably upset at the diagnosis and walked off to spend some time by himself, but even though I understand he knows Cambridge well, he could not remember where he was or where he was meant to be meeting your mother.'

Rose could remember it as though it were yesterday. The sunny April day as she sat by the banks of the Cam watching the punts and the rowboats drift by. She'd felt this wonderful sense of freedom, knowing she had finally done the right thing. She hadn't been aware of Lord Digby at first, she'd been so caught up in her own world, but after a few minutes of him pacing backwards and forwards she had noticed him.

'I met your father by the River Cam and I could see he was agitated. I managed to calm him down and eventually piece together where he could have left your mother. I walked with him up Silver Street to Trumpington Street and there was Lady Digby, frantic but ever so grateful.'

'She offered you a job.'

'Yes. She saw how I was with Lord Digby and said she admired how calm I had kept. At first the job was to be one of a housemaid, but if things went well, I think your mother was already thinking of the position I hold today.'

'It was a brave decision, taking a job with from a woman you did not know.'

'It was an easy decision. I had nothing of great substance waiting for me in London.' Rose shrugged. 'And I could tell Lady Digby was the sort of woman I would want to work for.'

'You seem to make up your mind about people very quickly.'

'I do.'

'Do you find your first impressions are generally right?'

'Most of the time.' She looked up at him and gave a wry smile. 'One day I'll tell you about my childhood and all the times I had to rely on my instincts to survive.'

Chapter Twelve

Richard sat watching Rose as she fussed around his father in the back of the carriage. They were on their way to Houghton Hall for the picnic Sebastian had suggested the day before. He was feeling unsettled and was finding it difficult to sit still, turning this way and that, crossing his arms and then uncrossing them. Thankfully the journey in the carriage was short, not allowing him too much time to think on what was to come.

Sebastian and his wife were standing out in front of their grand house, ready to greet their guests. They must have seen the horses making their way up the curving drive as they were waiting as soon as the house came into view from the window of the carriage.

Richard knew what was expected of him. He should step down from the carriage and greet his hosts, compliment them on their home and their children and talk about the weather and the latest local gossip. As he stepped down, he felt his whole body clench and tighten and he was glad he had the excuse of turning to support his father as he climbed down and then holding a hand out for Rose.

He turned, wondering if the panic was obvious in his eyes. His throat seemed as though it were closing and his tongue swelling in his mouth. Beside him, he felt Rose step a little closer and, unwitnessed by anyone else, she placed a hand in the small of his back, leaning into murmur something quietly. To an onlooker it would simply seem as if his father's caregiver was alerting him to some important information about the older man in her charge. In reality, her words were ones designed to pull him from the panic he was feeling.

'Be strong,' she said softly. 'Lady Cambridgeshire is holding out the hand of friendship despite what it might cost her emotionally. You should do the same.'

Sebastian stepped forward and clapped him on the back, then Richard was face to face with the woman he had known since childhood. The sister of the man he had killed.

'Lady Cambridgeshire, you look well,' Richard said, bowing low.

'As do you, Mr Digby. I swear you have not aged in the eight years since I last saw you.'

'I hear you have six wonderful children.'

'Yes, they are my pride and joy.'

'How is Elizabeth faring?'

'She is rallying. We were quite concerned for a few days, but Elizabeth is a strong girl. I think she will make a full recovery.'

'I am glad to hear it.'

Their conversation was polite but stilted and Richard

knew at some point he would have to acknowledge the huge issue that was sitting between them.

'Lord Digby, we are so pleased you could come to visit,' Lady Cambridgeshire said, beaming at the older man.

'Lovely house,' Lord Digby said, shaking Lord Cambridgeshire's hand. He looked small against the younger man, and although he was calm, Richard could see his father did not know where they were or why they were here.

'Come through to the garden. We have a comfortable chair and a delicious picnic set up, as long as the children have not raided it yet.'

Richard watched as Rose gently took his father's arm and led him through the house behind Lord and Lady Cambridgeshire. He had to admire her quiet resolve and her ability to take charge of a situation. Mr Watkins had accompanied them for the journey, but stayed in the carriage, ready to be called upon if anything was needed throughout the afternoon.

'Here,' Lady Cambridgeshire said, motioning to a beautifully laid-out area on the lawn at the back of Houghton Hall. There was a collection of chairs as well as a blanket laid out on the ground and cushions and rugs to make the whole area more comfortable.

'Let us find you a spot in the shade, my lord,' Rose said, helping Lord Digby select a chair and getting him settled into it comfortably. His father beamed up at the maid and gripped hold of her hand. There was trust in that gesture and an unspoken fear that he might be left alone in this unfamiliar place.

'Sit, Rose,' Richard said, lowering his voice so the Cambridgeshires did not hear his use of her given name.

'I do not want to intrude,' she said and he saw how uncomfortable she felt in this situation. She was neither guest nor normal maid. Her presence was required here, alongside Lord Digby, but that would mean attending a picnic with people on a different rung of the social ladder.

'It is no intrusion. You cannot be elsewhere, my father needs you, and there is no reason you should have to be uncomfortable for the next hour.'

Rose gave him a half-smile and sank down on to a cushion beside the chair, one of her hands still gripped tightly by Lord Digby.

'Please, make yourself comfortable, Mr Digby,' Lady Cambridgeshire said as she fussed over the cushions and rugs.

'Thank you. You have no objections to Miss Carpenter staying? She keeps my father calm.'

'Of course not,' Lady Cambridgeshire said, smiling beatifically at Rose. 'You are most welcome, my dear. My husband has told me what a help you have been to Lady Digby.'

'Thank you for your kindness, your ladyship,' Rose said.

They talked about the inconsequential for a while, touching on the weather, the floods of past winters, the expected new laws to be passed through Parliament in the coming year. Conversation was light and flowed easily, but Richard found himself completely on edge. It felt wrong to be sitting here enjoying himself, especially when he was in such close proximity to the sister of the man he had all but killed.

He was thankful when the food was brought out. A parade of footmen and maids brought plates piled high with cold meats and cheeses and bread alongside delicacies and cakes, arranging the platters on the nearby tables and then bringing things over one by one to serve to the guests. Richard was pleased to see Rose was handed a plate. Many people would not think to allow a servant to join in even an informal meal, but Lord and Lady Cambridgeshire were kind and all too aware that Rose would be sitting out here in the heat of the day without any refreshment if they did not provide some.

'This is good food,' Richard said as he bit into a salmon and pastry delicacy.

'A little different to what you must be used to,' Sebastian said. 'Tell us of your time away.'

Richard saw Rose put down her own plate and lean forward, as if eager to hear herself what his travels had been like.

'I was away a long time; I have been to many different places.'

'Tell us about your favourite,' Lady Cambridgeshire said, an encouraging smile on her face. It didn't feel right to be talking of what he had been doing these last few years, not when her brother was dead.

He shifted uncomfortably, but her eyes were boring into him and he knew he had to speak.

'I was in India when I heard about the eruption of Mount Tambora,' he said, looking out across the garden and picturing himself in the lush rainforest again. The eruption had happened a few weeks earlier and some merchants had brought news from that part of the world. 'I had helped to rebuild after a few earthquakes and hurricanes in South America and the West Indies and thought I might be able to make myself useful. An extra pair of hands is never turned away when there is so much work to be done.'

'You just decided to travel to the Dutch East Indies on the chance you would be able to help?' Lady Cambridgeshire said.

'Yes. I know it sounds conceited, that I thought my presence would make a difference. I was not trying to insert myself in the locals' tragedies and become some sort of saviour figure, I simply wanted to help.' He looked down, feeling his cheeks flush. He didn't want them to misunderstand his motives. 'I am young and fit and not afraid of physical labour, whereas many of the survivors were older or injured or unwell.'

'We do not think you inserted yourself into the situation to receive accolades,' Sebastian said, shaking his head. 'We know why you went.'

Richard frowned. Sometimes he found it hard to understand his own motivations. After Frederick Godrum's death he had first sought oblivion and anonymity, but that had not been enough. He had felt a need not for punishment exactly, but to make himself live in a way that allowed little pleasure. He ate only the blandest food, took on physically hard labour and slept on the thinnest mat in the most basic of accommodation. It had seemed the right way to live after what he had done.

Slowly, the idea of trying to do better, trying to give something good to the world, began to form. When he was caught up in the hurricane outside New York he had not left as many of the other visitors to the area had chosen to, he had stayed, helping to rebuild homes and shops, helping farmers to salvage what they could from their weather-beaten fields.

He had given his time and effort freely, living off the small allowance his investments gave him. Once the little town was recovering it had been time for him to move on and he realised that in the past months, helping the citizens of Travis, he had felt a modicum of peace. His nights were not haunted by images of Godrum's mutilated face and his days were not plagued by a guilt so overwhelming he could hardly move.

So, he had moved on, travelling through the country for a while, feeling a growing unease when there was not a focus to his time. When he heard of a tropical storm that had battered one of the islands in the West Indies, he had organised a passage, rented a small room and helped with the process of clearing up the debris from the storm.

It had been a pattern he repeated time and again over the years, drifting for a while until he found a focus for his energies and then working hard for a few months to help rebuild after a tragedy. He stayed to help while help was needed, moving on before he could put down roots.

'So much had been destroyed on the island from the eruption, not just from the lava flow, but from the fires that had spread far and wide. Then there was the famine.'

Richard pressed his lips together. It had been the worst disaster he had ever seen, not purely because of the total destruction caused by the initial eruption, but also because of the cloud of ash that had risen up and blocked out the sun for months and months. On his return journey to England he had learned the effects of the eruption had been far-reaching, leading to a poor harvest across much of the world as temperatures stayed far lower than usual and the sky was covered by a persistent ash cloud.

'By the time I arrived in the Dutch East Indies the main threat was the lack of food. Crops had been destroyed and there was no hope of a new harvest. In the area I settled, one of the village leaders had a plan to venture out and increase trade with the Dutch, but there was a certain animosity between the locals and the Dutch. I offered my assistance and acted as an intermediary. It was different work to what I normally did, but they did not need me to help with rebuilding homes and public buildings, so I did what I could.'

'What a terrible disaster,' Lady Cambridgeshire said, a hand covering her mouth. 'We read about it in the papers, of course, many months after it had happened, and spared a thought for those killed in the eruption, but you do not think of the after-effects.'

'That can be the most dangerous time. Initially, some of the other islands sent some aid, but once the fires were out and the dead buried, other people moved on and had their own famine to deal with.'

'How did you communicate with them?' Sebastian said, looking at him with interest.

'With difficulty. In South America and the West Indies many people know a little English or Spanish, and I learned enough Spanish to be able to communicate the basics, but this was a different language entirely. As we worked the locals taught me how to speak their language word by word, pointing things out and howling with laughter at my pronunciation until I got the words right. I am by no means fluent, but by the end of the eight months I spent there I could work out what was needed.'

'You always were a clever one,' Sebastian said.

Richard turned to Lady Cambridgeshire and wondered if he should say more. He was acutely conscious of the precarious balance here. He wanted her to see he was doing whatever he could to make a positive impact in the world, but he also didn't want her to think that he thought he could make up for what he had done to her brother.

'If Sebastian hadn't called you home, what was the plan next?' Lady Cambridgeshire said before he could speak.

'I don't know. I think I would have spent a few more months there and then started to wander again.'

'Do people live very differently there, Mr Digby?' Rose said, her eyes shining as she leaned forward.

'Yes, they do, in a practical sense. Their houses are built differently and there is more of a focus on producing what is needed to live rather than on the material. The women will make their own clothes, the men will fashion their own implements for fishing or hunting, but people are essentially the same wherever you are in the world. Their ways of life might be different, but they still love their families, they have hopes and fears and vices.'

He smiled softly, remembering one of the children who often used to follow him around while he was helping to distribute the grain that had arrived on a boat in the harbour. 'The games the children play look different on the surface, but when you watch carefully, they are no different to the make-believe worlds of children from all parts of the globe.'

'Is it beautiful?' Rose asked, and for a moment Richard forgot they were sitting with Lord and Lady Cambridgeshire; his words were directed solely at Rose.

'More beautiful than you can imagine. There are long stretches of pristine white sand, with the turquoise blue of the ocean on one side and palm trees lining the other. The interior is hilly, sometimes mountainous, and so lush. The locals mainly live close to the beach in small settlements as they fish as one of their main sources of food, but they also farm the verdant slopes.'

It had been beautiful, but a very tragic sort of beauty. He had arrived in the Dutch East Indies a considerable amount of time after the eruption, but the devastation was ongoing. The natural beauty of the islands was still evident, but it was hard to see it when the population had been so decimated. Over time the people on the islands would recover, but those who had lived on the slopes of Mount Tambora had been all but wiped out, whole families disappeared in a few moments of tragedy.

'It must have been dangerous,' Lady Cambridgeshire said, her eyes narrowing a little as she addressed him. 'The threat of the volcano, the lack of food and dozens of untold perils.'

'It was not the safest place,' Richard conceded. He didn't mention the very real threat of the diseases that had spread through the islands in the aftermath of the eruption. Water had been contaminated and people were frail from the lack of food.

'Yet you chose to go there,' Lady Cambridgeshire pressed him and Richard shifted uncomfortably.

'I thought I could do something to help someone,' he said quietly. 'Even if it made a difference to just one person, surely that is worth it. I made sure I did not consume more than I contributed, I dug wells and irrigation channels. I made sure I was never a burden to any of the communities I stayed in.

'I was all too aware of the danger of trying to assuage my guilt by inserting myself into other people's tragedies, thinking I was making a difference, but instead making things harder by eating their food, drinking their water and slowing them down, but I do not think that happened.'

'I am sure they were happy to have a strong, healthy man to help shoulder some of their burdens,' Lady Cambridgeshire said, giving him a faint smile. 'I am not doubting that. I suppose I am lamenting the fact you felt driven there in the first place.' She stood abruptly, mumbling an apology, and then dashed off in the direction of the house. Sebastian gave Richard an apologetic shrug and then rose and followed his wife.

He let his head sag and squeezed his eyes tight shut. This was not going well. After a moment he felt a soft hand on his shoulder.

'You should talk to her,' Rose said softly.

'I was talking to her,' he snapped.

'I mean properly talk to her.'

'It won't help,' he said quietly, aware of his father

sitting a few feet away, although the old man wasn't taking much interest in their conversation.

'These are your friends; they care about you.'

'Lady Cambridgeshire is a good woman, a generous woman, but how can she feel anything but hatred towards me?'

'Perhaps she doesn't blame you for what happened.'

He scoffed at the idea and shook his head.

'Perhaps she is more forgiving than you,' Rose ventured again. His head snapped up and his eyes met hers. 'Do not deny it,' she said, her voice firm. 'You have done nothing but punish yourself for what happened at the duel for the last eight years.'

'So, what if I have? I was responsible for my friend's death, Rose. I do not deserve Lady Cambridgeshire's kindness or her friendship.'

'You do not get to decide that. If she wishes to bestow it, you do not have the right to deny her that comfort.'

Richard let his head drop forward and considered Rose's words. He still felt a simmering irritation towards her. She only knew what he had told her, she hadn't lived with the guilt and the image of Frederick Godrum in his last moments for the past eight years. Yet something she said resonated inside him. Perhaps she was right—it wasn't up to him to decide how Lady Cambridgeshire felt or how she wanted to act towards him.

For a long moment he was silent and then he nodded. 'I will talk to Lady Cambridgeshire,' he said.

Rose watched as Mr Digby paced backwards and forward across the lawn. She could see his lips moving and the frown on his face even from her seat twenty feet away. Beside her, Lord Digby let out a soft snore as he dozed in the comfortable chair, his head lolling to one side. She leaned over and gently adjusted his position, so he was better supported, and then returned to watching Mr Digby.

She felt a deep sympathy for him. In every action, every sentence you could hear the guilt he felt and the perpetual punishment he thought he deserved. It was not a healthy way to live and she didn't doubt he had put himself in danger more than once in the time he had been away. If he carried on living the same sort of life, one day his luck would run out.

She watched Lord and Lady Cambridgeshire emerge from the house and start to make their way across the garden towards their guests. Mr Digby stepped forward and intercepted Lady Cambridgeshire and she saw with satisfaction that after exchanging a few words, the Countess nodded in agreement and then took Mr Digby's arm.

'Do I sense your intervention, Miss Carpenter?' Lord Cambridgeshire said as he came and sat beside her, picking up one of the heavy painted iron chairs and carrying it a little closer.

'You think a maid would have influence over the son of a baron?'

Lord Cambridgeshire smiled at her and shook his head ruefully.

'I have never been a stickler for the hierarchies in society,' he said, reaching out and taking a strawberry tart from the tray on the table. 'And I think you are a kindred spirit in that regard, are you not, Miss Carpenter?'

'I have been dismissed from a position before be-cause my mistress did not think I knew my place, my lord,' Rose said. She liked Lord Cambridgeshire and his genial personality. Of course they had very little common ground and he was one of the wealthiest and most important men in the country, but he treated her as a person, always greeting her when he came to visit Lord and Lady Digby.

'Well, I am very glad you overstepped today, Miss Carpenter. I do not know what you said to Mr Digby, but I don't think he would be over there talking to my wife if you had not prompted him.'

Rose was silent for a moment. 'Were you there?' It was a risky question to ask and it could sour the mood of their conversation.

Lord Cambridgeshire silently shook his head. 'No. I wish I had been. Frederick was a good friend of mine, but he did not know of the attachment between Ame-lia and myself. If I had been there...' He trailed off and closed his eyes for a moment. 'Guilt is a terrible thing,' he said quietly. 'I carry the guilt of knowing every day that if I had been open about my intentions with Amelia, Frederick would probably not have interpreted Digby's actions so poorly and the duel would never have hap-pened. I think there are many of us that wish we could turn back the clock, but it is impossible, of course.'

'Impossible,' Rose agreed. 'Your wife is very brave, wanting to mend things between her and Mr Digby.'

'She is. Lady Cambridgeshire is a generous woman, but in this case, it is not her kind, sweet spirit that pushes her to reach out to Digby. She does not blame him for her brother's death. Frederick was always impulsive, always doing things that would get him into trouble. Lady Cambridgeshire knows Digby fired up into the air, she knows her brother's pistol misfired and he was foolish enough to turn the barrel and look down it. *None* of that is Digby's fault.'

'He thinks he should have put aside his pride and found some way to prevent the duel from happening.'

Lord Cambridgeshire scoffed and shook his head. 'Impossible. They were both proud young men who thought they were invincible.'

'They certainly weren't invincible.' She paused, wondering whether to ask the next question. 'Mr Digby said Mr Godrum's father threatened him with dire consequences if he ever came back to England—do you think that is still a risk?'

'Old Mr Godrum was a bastard—excuse my language.'

Rose smiled. Her early years had been filled with nothing but bad language. Drunks and villains did not think to moderate their foul mouths around children, especially not filthy street urchins.

'He had a malicious streak, but he did love Frederick in his own way. He was one of those that cares only for their sons, for the heir who will carry on the family name. When Frederick died, it left only Amelia and he was furious his heir had been taken from him.'

'He sounds delightful,' Rose murmured.

'Digby went to see the Godrums, to tell them what had happened. I think he needed to look them in the eye and tell them how truly sorry he was. Old Mr Godrum told him that he would never be forgiven, not in this life or the next, and if Digby stayed in England, he would do everything in his power to have him prosecuted for the duelling and anything else he could throw at him.'

'I suppose he had just lost his son. Grief can be terrible.'

'It can and I think no one would have blamed the Godrums for making threats at that time. Everything was so raw, so fresh.'

'What about now?'

'Old Mr Godrum died a few years ago.'

'And Mrs Godrum?'

'She is not like her husband. When Mr Godrum was alive, she was cowed into agreeing with everything her husband said, but now...' he shook his head '...she is much more reasonable.'

'You do not think she would rush to press the authorities to arrest Mr Digby.'

'No,' Lord Cambridgeshire said without hesitation. 'Certainly not. And I do not think anyone would be interested in charging him with duelling when the offence happened so long ago.'

'Good. At least it is one less reason for him to leave the country.'

They fell silent as Lord Digby stirred next to Rose, but after opening his eyes for a moment he slowly drifted back to sleep.

Chapter Thirteen

'Do not fret, Miss Carpenter, we will take good care of Lord Digby,' Lord Cambridgeshire said.

Beside her husband, Lady Cambridgeshire smiled encouragingly. Lord Digby was dozing in his chair still, content and quiet in the shade. He would likely sleep for at least another half an hour, but still she felt guilty for abandoning him.

'Come, Rose,' Mr Digby said softly, 'it will do no harm to enjoy yourself for a few minutes. Even the most dedicated workers need a little break from time to time.'

He offered her his arm and after a moment's hesitation she took it and allowed him to lead her on a gentle stroll through the gardens.

'I know these grounds almost as well as the land surrounding Meadow View,' Mr Digby said as they walked past the rose beds and followed a path through a gate into an orchard. There were row upon row of apple trees stretching out in all directions, bees buzzing from one tree to the next in an idyllic countryside scene.

'Lord Cambridgeshire and I were inseparable,' he

explained as he led her through the trees. 'I would beg my mother to bring me over here and then Sebastian and I would disappear in the garden for hours.'

It was a very different childhood to the one she had experienced, but Rose didn't begrudge him his fond memories. She could imagine him as a boy, running through the orchard with wooden sword in hand, engaged in some make-believe game with his best friend. It was a happy scene, one of innocence and pure joy, before tragedy had struck and his path had changed for ever.

'What would you play, Mr Digby?'

'All sorts. We went through a pirate and smuggler phase for a long time—I would be the pirate and Sebastian the man trying to capture me. It was an elaborate game of hide and seek, I suppose, but it kept us entertained for hours.'

'Where would you hide?'

Mr Digby smiled at her and she saw a flash of the carefree boy he once must have been. Before she could utter a word of caution, he reached up and grabbed hold of the branch of a sturdy apple tree above their heads and pulled himself up as if it were no effort at all. She watched in astonishment as he swung a leg over and straddled the branch, leaning back against the trunk of the tree.

'They have something ridiculous like two thousand trees on the land around Houghton Hall—Sebastian used to have trouble finding me.'

'I can't believe you climbed up there,' Rose said, still looking up at him.

'Care to join me?'

She looked at the branch dubiously. It was well above her head and, although she could stretch to reach it, there was no way she would ever be able to pull herself up.

'I'll never get up there.'

For a moment, she thought he might suggest he help her up, but after a moment he shrugged and slipped to the ground, landing softly on his feet and brushing himself down.

'Let me take you somewhere else instead,' he said. Quickly, he led her through the orchard, weaving a path to another door in the wall opposite the one they had come through from the garden. This door was shut and locked, the rusty iron handle not budging, even with a good rattle.

'I suppose we should turn back,' Rose said, starting to walk away.

'No need. If I remember correctly, there should be a key.' He reached up, stretching to feel in a small alcove above the gate and shouting out in triumph as his fingers tightened around something and pulled it down. It was an ancient key, elaborate and heavy in design, as rusty as the handle, but in working condition as he slotted it into the lock.

'Do you think Lord and Lady Cambridgeshire will mind us unlocking their gate?'

'No, not at all. It is still their land beyond. I expect they keep it locked to ensure the children don't have an easy path to the river.' He led her through the gate, closed it and locked it behind him, pocketing the key. 'We'll lock it again once we come back through and put the key back then.'

They were close to the river now, the water burbling only a few feet away. There was a wide path along the banks that ran along the outer wall of the orchard.

'It's beautiful, isn't it?' Mr Digby said and Rose was glad to see him smiling.

He seemed relaxed here with his friends, even after the intense talk he'd had with Lady Cambridgeshire and the reservations he'd fostered about coming into her home when she might hold him at least partially responsible for the death of her brother. It spoke of the goodness and generosity of his friends that they could still put him at ease despite everything that had happened between them.

'I have not travelled far in my life, but I do not think I have seen anywhere more beautiful than the River Great Ouse surrounded by wildflowers in summer.'

'Do you trust me, Rose?' Mr Digby said, holding out his hand for her.

'Trust you?'

'I want to take you on the water, but I know after your dip the other day you might be nervous.'

'What do you mean? How will you take me on the water?'

'Look.' He led her along the bank a few feet to a bend in the river and motioned to a small rowboat that was tethered to a weather-worn pole. 'The river is calm and shallow. I do not think there is any danger whatsoever, Rose.'

She bit her lip, remembering the panic she had felt a few days earlier when she had fallen into the cold water. It was terrifying not being able to swim, even if the river was shallow enough to stand in, but she saw the look of anticipation on Mr Digby's face and realised she could not turn down his offer.

It was the first time she had seen him so relaxed, so at ease. Perhaps it was not having the worry about his father or perhaps it was because he had faced Lady Cambridgeshire and had one less thing to ruminate about, worrying if she would rather he disappeared from her life entirely. It was as though a small part of him had been liberated and he wanted to celebrate by showing her some of the things he used to enjoy.

'It is safe?'

'Completely.'

'You have never capsized before?'

He hesitated. 'I cannot lie, I have capsized many a time, but that was when Sebastian and I were fooling around. I promise to be completely sensible the whole time we are on the water.'

'Then I accept your offer.'

He smiled at her, and Rose felt her heart squeeze in her chest. Quickly, she dismissed the feeling, telling herself not to be so foolish. He was trying to share something wholesome with her, something from his childhood, a happier time. The last thing she needed was to imagine him leaning over while they were in the boat and kissing her.

She stood on the bank while he untied the rope that secured the little wooden vessel and readied the oars and then he turned, placing one foot on the bank and one in the boat to steady it, reaching out to offer her a hand. Rose gripped hold of him, trying to ignore the pounding in her chest as she stepped from the bank. In her fear, she stumbled a little, but Mr Digby's grip was firm, and as she stepped down he pulled her to his chest, holding her close until she found her balance.

Swallowing hard, she glanced up at him. His expression was one of concern and she wanted to cling on to him for longer, to feel the reassurance of his arms around her for more than just a few seconds, but she knew it was not an option. Instead, she slowly released him, making sure she was steady before moving to one of the little benches and sitting down.

The boat rocked alarmingly as Mr Digby got himself settled and slotted the oars into place and she clung to the bench as if it were the only thing keeping her from a watery grave.

'Ready?'

She nodded, not trusting her voice to stay level, and forced herself to breathe deeply as they pushed away from the banks.

The river truly was shallow here, the water running clear and giving a good view of the plants that grew from the bottom, oscillating in the current.

'We won't go far. I seem to remember there is a pretty little bridge a few hundred feet upriver. Perhaps we can row there and then let the current bring us back.'

As some of her trepidation left her, Rose watched Mr Digby with interest. He was rowing against the current, but despite the effort to move the little rowing boat he tackled the task with ease. After a minute he paused, leaning the oars against his legs, and slipped off his jacket, rolling up his shirtsleeves and loosening the cravat about his neck.

Rose pressed her lips together, telling herself it was rude to stare. Despite the silent reprimand she was unable to tear her eyes away from Mr Digby's tanned forearms as they worked the oars. For a moment, she remembered how his arms had felt as they encircled her body when he had steadied her, holding her close to him. Quickly, she dismissed the thought. All Mr Digby was trying to do was enjoy the peaceful summer's afternoon and share some of that enjoyment with her, too.

'You've never been in a boat before?' Mr Digby enquired as he got back to the work of pulling them up-river.

'Never. Not even on the Thames. I must admit it is not as unpleasant as I expected.'

'I suppose it is not the ideal form of transport if you are scared of the water.'

'I'm not scared of the water,' she said indignantly. 'I can walk by a river quite happily as long as I know there's no chance of falling in.'

'Perhaps if you plan to continue to live in this part of Cambridgeshire, surrounded by water, you should think about learning to swim.'

She scoffed. 'It is hardly as simple as that.'

'Why not?'

'You don't simply wake up one day and declare you are going to learn to swim, then find the nearest pond or river to jump into.'

This elicited a smile from Mr Digby.

'Perhaps not quite like that. I would suggest maybe having someone who can swim accompany you.'

'And who would you suggest, Mr Digby? Your mother, perhaps? Or Mrs Green, the cook? Or perhaps one of the stable boys?'

He shook his head and laughed. 'I see your dilemma.

There is no one suitable.' He paused for a second and then held her eye. 'I could teach you.'

Rose felt the heat flood to her cheeks at the idea of slipping into the water with Mr Digby.

'Luckily I have no intention of actually learning to swim so I will not hold you to that offer.'

'I think it would be quite fun. We could find a shallow pool somewhere.'

'Imagine the scandal,' Rose murmured, shaking her head. 'The whole of Cambridgeshire would be convinced you had contracted some terrible disease from your travels that had turned you quite mad and robbed you of all sense.'

'I am sure they would, Rose, but perhaps it would be worth it if you could swim at the end of it.'

'You feel so strongly about water safety.'

'I feel strongly about not feeling fear for such a wonderful part of nature.'

They fell silent, Rose trying hard not to contemplate what an hour spent in a secluded pool with Mr Digby might be like.

'Tell me, Rose, do you plan on staying here in Cambridgeshire?'

'I think so, for a while at least.'

'My mother will be pleased.'

'I do not know what will happen once…' She trailed off, not wanting to put Lord Digby's inevitable death into words.

'Once my father passes away?'

She nodded. 'I do not know if there will be a place for me.'

'My mother is a loyal woman; she would not see anyone out of a job if she could help it.'

'I know, she is a wonderful mistress, yet circumstances change. None of us knows what our lives will look like in five years' time, or ten.'

'That is true,' he said, his eyes sliding away from hers, and she wondered if he was thinking about how his life was not how he had imagined growing up. After a moment he rallied and fixed her with a breezy smile. Rose could see it didn't quite reach his eyes, but he was trying not to dwell too much on his past and she appreciated his effort. 'Let us not think of the practicalities, but tell me what you would do if every option in the world was open to you?'

She laughed. 'That is a game of the wealthy. Those of us born into the lower classes have no time to fantasise. We are all too busy scrubbing chamber pots or polishing our masters' silver.'

'I do not believe it,' he said quietly. 'I think everyone dreams, from the poorest beggar on the streets to the Prince Regent himself. I think everyone has that secret thought of what they would do if they were totally free.'

'What is yours?' Rose asked quickly.

Mr Digby pondered for a moment, resting the oars on his thighs as he looked out over the riverbank into the distance.

'If I was truly free, I would want a life of domesticity. Surrounded by family, happy in a comfortable house. It makes me sound terribly dull, doesn't it?'

She shook her head and realised he had given her a genuine answer.

'When you have been absent for so long, moving

around from place to place, it makes you realise what is important in this life. How about you, Rose?'

For a minute, she considered her answer, wanting to be as honest with him as he had been with her. 'If I had all the money I could need, safety and comfort so I did not have to work, I would start a school for the children of the slums in London.'

'That is an admirable answer.'

She shook her head. 'Not admirable, just the truth. Of course, I would like to travel, to see far-flung shores and experience places I can only dream of and to do so surrounded by people I love, but more than that I would like to leave this world knowing that I have done something to help the poor children left scraping an existence on the streets of London.'

They had reached the little bridge Mr Digby had mentioned and he hauled up the oars, letting them rest on the edge of the boat, the paddles lifted above the water. Slowly, they began to drift back downstream. Every so often he would dip one of the oars back into the water to help adjust their course, but otherwise he let the current transport them.

'I hope one day you might get to realise that dream.'

'I am aware it is highly unlikely. Growing up as I did makes you realise there are far worse things than a hard day's work. I do not mind my life now, Mr Digby.'

He smiled at her, but she saw a hint of sadness about him again.

'I am glad. It is not often you come across someone who is happy with their lot in life.'

They drifted in silence for a while, Rose relaxing enough to lean back a little and allow her fingers to trail over the surface of the water, creating ripples that spread out far and wide from their rowboat.

In no time at all they were back to the little mooring post close to the high walls of the orchard. Rose felt a tug of disappointment that their little interlude together was almost over, but she knew they must return to Lord Digby. He might still be dozing in the sun, but if he woke without a familiar face to calm him, he would soon become agitated.

She was more confident as she stood this time, feeling the rocking of the wood underneath her feet, but not panicking, instead allowing her body to sway with the movement so she did not overbalance.

'I think you are already well on your way to developing a love of the water,' Mr Digby said as he hopped from the boat and began tying it up. Only once it was fully secure did he lean back over and offer her his hand.

'It has been a very pleasant half an hour,' Rose said as he pulled her up to the riverbank. 'Thank you, Mr Digby.'

For a long moment they stood close together, Mr Digby still holding on to her hand. Rose felt the thrum of desire pass between them, but this time she didn't immediately step away. She was intrigued by this man who initially seemed as if he wanted to push everyone away, but underneath that stony exterior lay a thoughtful and considerate heart.

She didn't want to break away first, aware that once they walked back through the orchard they would fall into their prescribed roles and lose the closeness she now felt. She knew it was ridiculous—she was a servant and he the son of her mistress, yet still she found it hard to step away.

'Thank you for your company this afternoon, Rose. It has been a sublime half an hour.'

Chapter Fourteen

It was a little after ten o'clock and for once Lord Digby had settled easily, taking to his bed without any protestations when Rose had suggested he might be tired. She had sat with him for a while, listening to his deep, even breathing, only rising when she could be certain he was completely settled.

She planned to take Lord Digby's shirts that needed washing downstairs and then go to bed herself. It had been a successful day, with Lord Digby enjoying the change in scenery more than she had expected him to, but it had been tiring to always be alert, never knowing how her master would react to the different people and places.

'Is he settled?' Mr Digby called as Rose passed the study. She paused, poking her head round the door.

'Yes, he's fast asleep.'

'Come in here, Rose.'

She stepped into the room and was surprised when Mr Digby got up from behind his desk and came over to meet her.

'I have a surprise for you,' he said.

He'd been quiet in the carriage on the way back from the picnic. After they had rejoined Lord and Lady Cambridgeshire, they had stayed for half an hour more until Lord Digby awoke from his after-lunch sleep and then had quickly said their goodbyes. Lady Cambridgeshire had embraced Mr Digby before he had left and made him promise to visit again soon, and Rose fancied she had seen the sheen of tears in his eyes, although she knew he would never admit such a weakness.

They had travelled in silence in the carriage with all attempts at conversation halted by Mr Digby's monosyllabic answers to her questions. When they had arrived back at Meadow View he had hopped down from the carriage, assisted her and Mr Watkins with getting Lord Digby out and up to his rooms, before disappearing without a word.

'A surprise?'

'Yes, to say thank you.'

Rose raised her eyebrows. 'Thank you? What for?'

'For encouraging me to talk to Lady Cambridgeshire.'

'It was a worthwhile talk?'

'Yes.'

He didn't elaborate further and Rose wasn't sure she wanted to push him.

'I am pleased.'

'I was too absorbed in my own feelings to realise hers should come first.'

'No—' Rose began to say, but Mr Digby continued before she could say any more.

'I need to put her feelings above my own. She is the one who matters.'

'No,' Rose said more vehemently.

Mr Digby looked at her, perplexed. 'What do you mean, no? It was what you said to me when we were in Lord and Lady Cambridgeshire's.'

'I said you needed to consider her opinion, her feelings.'

'And that is what I did.'

'I did not say her feelings should come above yours.'

'Of course they should.'

Rose closed her eyes in frustration. She wanted to grip his shoulder, to shake him and tell him he was a person, too, someone who deserved not to suppress their emotions to make others more comfortable.

'She lost her brother, Rose. I was the reason she lost her brother. Of course her feelings are more important than mine.'

'No,' Rose said sharply, giving in to the urge that had been building and reaching out for him. She gripped him hard, her fingers digging into his skin through the layers of shirt and jacket and shook him. 'You cannot dismiss yourself so easily.'

Before he looked away, Rose saw the same thing she had seen earlier in the day before the picnic. She wasn't quite sure what it was—perhaps defeat, perhaps self-loathing—but it was not healthy. It pained her to see him think of himself in such a way.

After he had first spoken to Lady Cambridgeshire, when they had taken the stroll through the orchard and spent the time in the rowboat on the river, he had seemed positive about the conversation between him and his friend's wife. There had been something almost celebratory about him, as if he was finally going to start forgiving himself, but Rose could see now he had mused on Lady Cambridgeshire's words, pulled them apart and found new meaning.

'You have to forgive yourself,' she said softly, knowing her words would not get through, but needing to try anyway. 'You must let go of this guilt. It will kill you.'

'Maybe that is what I deserve.'

'No. You don't believe that, not deep down.'

He took a long, shuddering breath and then shook his head. 'In my darkest moments I have believed that, but I do not now. It would be pointless—dying will not bring Frederick back, it will not atone for what I did. While I am alive, I can try to do some good and that at least is worthwhile.'

'You cannot live like this,' Rose said, reaching up from his shoulder with one hand and placing it on his cheek. It was an intimate gesture and Rose was aware she had trampled over the boundary that was supposed to separate master and servant, but right now she couldn't find it in herself to care. Every time she looked at him, she saw a man suffering, a man crying out for comfort even though he would never admit it. She could give that comfort.

His eyes locked on to hers and she felt a pulse of attraction pass between them. For a long moment neither of them moved and Rose's fingers felt as though they were burning where they made contact with his skin.

'Rose,' he said and sounded like a man who was drowning.

She stepped closer so their bodies were almost touching as his hand came up and covered hers, pressing it to his cheek.

'You deserve some happiness,' she said, her voice barely more than a whisper.

Her chest rose and fell rapidly and inside her body her blood pulsed quickly through her veins. She felt her cheeks flush and every part of her felt on edge, as if waiting for something spectacular to happen.

When Mr Digby leaned forward and kissed her, she felt her legs tense to stop them from buckling and was grateful for the arm he looped around her waist. For a blissful moment there was nothing but the soft lips of the man in front of her. Rose felt her whole body sway and press against Mr Digby's and for the first time in a very long time she felt warm in the embrace of another.

The kiss was long and deep, full of passion and emotion, and Rose had never experienced anything like it. She felt as though Mr Digby were drawing her into his depths, claiming her as his own, never to relinquish her. In the moment the idea excited her and she fervently wished the moment would never end.

It was inevitable that the kiss was going to end, but Rose kept her eyes closed in the desperate hope that she might prolong it. Only when her lashes fluttered open and her eyes locked with Mr Digby's did the spell break. She felt him stiffen and then pull away, looking at her, aghast.

It was not the reaction any woman dreamed of and Rose felt a stab of pain run through her chest and into her heart.

For a long moment neither of them moved or spoke. They were standing only inches apart, both breathing rapidly, both desperately trying to understand what had just happened.

'Rose,' he said eventually, 'I am sorry, that was unforgivable.' His posture was stiff and his voice had a clipped edge to it.

She turned away first, unable to cope with the maelstrom of emotions that were fighting for prominence inside her. Kissing Mr Digby had never been the plan when she had reached out for him. She had wanted to ensure he was listening to her and to convey the importance of what she was saying, but as soon as her hands had reached out it had set off a chain of events that had made the kiss inevitable.

'Rose,' he said again, but she did not turn, holding up a finger, begging him to give her a moment to compose herself.

This was not where she wanted her relationship with Mr Digby to go. She had planned to offer friendship, if a maid could be friends with her mistress's son. After seeing his pain earlier in the day, she had thought to try to help him through it, the way Lady Digby had helped her when she had arrived, broken and desperate, at Meadow View two years ago.

She closed her eyes and took a deep breath. She shouldn't be hurt Mr Digby had looked at her with such horror—it was exactly the right reaction to have. Any developing feelings she had for him needed to be crushed straight away. This was exactly the sort of situation she had promised herself never to get into again. Although very different to her affair with Mr Rampton, father to the two children she had been nanny to, it would end the same way, in disaster.

There was too much imbalance with him holding all the power and her vulnerable to his every whim. What was more, she valued this position too much to do anything to jeopardise it. Lady Digby had helped Rose build her sense of self-worth again—through quiet kindness, she had made Rose realise not all employers would take advantage of their servants. That was too important to risk ruining her life for a kiss.

She turned and saw the despair on Mr Digby's face. Right now, she could not coax him through it. She knew he would be berating himself for giving in to the desire that flowed through him, for even thinking for one moment that he deserved the temporary bliss a passionate kiss could give.

'That was a mistake,' Rose said, so he wouldn't have to. She saw the relief blossom on his face and realised this was another reason nothing could ever happen between them. After her time with Mr Rampton, she had promised herself that if she ever did seek out a relationship again, she would only be with someone who would love her without limit, without any caveat.

Part of her was still broken from the way Mr Rampton had used her for his own pleasure, without giving anything back emotionally. Mr Digby was different, but he was still not able to love her, not when he had so much grief and guilt pent up inside him stopping him from living his life. 'We both agree it was a mistake.'

'It was unforgivable, Rose.'

She held up a hand and shook her head. 'Your conscience cannot take another thing you are punishing yourself for. Do not add this to it. It was a mistake, an overheated moment, that is all. I suggest we forget it ever happened and continue as we have been. I do not want to have to avoid your company and I certainly do not want to add to the burden you carry.'

'A mistake,' he murmured, nodding in agreement.

'An innocent mistake. One we both made. No one person is responsible.'

'I am in a position of power...'

'And I am perfectly capable of dealing with unwanted advances,' Rose said firmly. 'If I had not wanted to kiss you, *in that moment*, I would not have kissed you. You would have received a firm knee to the groin and, in all likelihood, you would still be rolling around on the floor in agony.'

This made him smile, and Rose felt a pang of regret. In another world, in another life, she could see them having a very different relationship. Despite initially finding him stiff and formal, Mr Digby was a genuine man and she found pleasure in his company. Perhaps if they had both been born to a different station and their paths had crossed, they would have had a chance at a normal courtship.

'I am sorry, Rose,' he said again, taking a step forward, then catching himself. 'That *was* unforgivable, especially after you told me what you went through with your old master.'

'You are not like him.'

'No, but it is still a position you should not have been put into.'

Rose forced a breezy smile on to her face. All she wanted to do was run away and hide in the sanctuary of her room, but if she did that the relationship with Mr Digby would always be strained. She needed to stay here and pretend she was not affected by what had happened.

'Perhaps not, but we both are equally to blame. Now, shall we forget about it?'

'It shall be as if it never happened.' He said the words, but at that moment Rose could see he didn't believe them.

'You said you had a surprise for me.'

'Yes, although I will understand if you did not want to go through with it tonight.'

'Show me the surprise, Mr Digby.'

He hesitated only a moment, then led the way out of the study into the dining room. Set out on the table was a light supper, beautifully prepared, with an open bottle of wine and two glasses.

'Perhaps not the best idea now,' he said with a wry smile. 'It looks as though I'm trying to seduce you.'

'Was that the plan?'

'No, it wasn't. I thought I would show my appreciation by sharing a meal with you and one of the finest bottles of wine in my father's collection.'

She could see what he had been trying to do, bridging the gap between them. Despite his unconventional living situation these last few years, it was hard to forget he was the son of a baron and one day in the not-too-distant future he would inherit Meadow View and the wealth the Digby family had amassed over generations.

In comparison, she was a maid, destined to work hard, long hours for the rest of her life. Already she had pulled herself up from the gutter and avoided the life many orphans born on London's streets faced, but she was realistic in knowing there was a ceiling above her and she would not be able to rise much further.

'Thank you,' she said, sitting down. She appreciated the gesture, but now more than ever she felt the gulf between them. It would be nothing short of foolish to think they could be friends.

They ate in silence for a moment, the awkwardness stretching out between them. She kept seeing Mr Digby's horrified face when he had pulled away from the kiss and knew, whatever she told herself, that wound would hurt for a while.

Richard knew he should say something, anything, to fill the awkward silence, but his mind was still reeling. If he was completely honest with himself, he could admit the attraction and desire had been building between him and Rose for a while. There was something about her that made him want to draw her closer, to disregard the differences in their social stations and follow the yearning he felt deep inside. Every time she came close, he felt the hypnotic pull of her deep brown eyes and had to resist the urge to reach out and touch her.

Tonight had been too much. When she had reached out and grazed his cheek with her fingers, he had not been able to think of anything but kissing her. Every reason it was a bad idea deserted him and he was left with the overwhelming urge to pull her close and make her his own.

In that moment of the kiss it had been blissful. For the first time in years, he felt as though the weight he carried was lifted from his shoulders. He thought nothing of the past or the future, only of her lips brushing against his.

Now he was almost overcome by guilt and regret, and by a terrible frustration, too. Kissing Rose had been unforgivable, especially with what he knew about her old master. Richard was in a position of power and he should know better than to abuse that, but he had not been able to resist as her body had pressed against his own.

As she sat there across from him, sipping on the wine, he wondered for a moment what life would be like if he allowed himself to fall in love. He had this wonderful image of tumbling into bed with Rose at the end of a long and satisfying day, his guilt over his past crimes lifted, allowing him to enjoy a full and satisfying life. It was never going to happen, but for a moment it was good to indulge in the fantasy.

'You said you would tell me about your childhood,' he said, reaching for any safe topic of conversation.

'I am not sure you want to hear about it, it is not the most uplifting of tales.'

'You are an orphan?'

'Yes, my parents died when I was young, my mother first and then my father a few years later.'

'Did you have relatives who took you in?'

'At first, but my extended family did not have much money. I would stay with an aunt for a while and then, when circumstances changed, I would be turned out to fend for myself until someone else took pity on me.'

'How old were you?'

'Five.'

'Five?' he repeated, incredulous. 'No five-year-old can survive on the streets of London by themselves.'

She held out her hands. 'I am proof that they can. I was not on the streets the whole time. There was a church orphanage that I lived in for a while and various relatives would keep me for a few months at a time, especially if they thought I could be useful.'

'What five-year-old can be useful?'

She shrugged. 'I looked innocent.'

'Innocent?'

'My job was to stand in the middle of the street and cry, create a fuss. When some well-to-do lady or gentleman stopped to see if they could assist a lost young child, my uncle would sweep in and pick their pocket.'

Richard's eyes widened, realising quite how dire Rose's young life must have been. He knew that thousands of people lived that way, especially in the cities, but it was a world apart from his own upbringing and difficult to think about a child in such awful circumstances.

'As I got older my uncle taught me to pick pockets. People are cautious around a hulking thirty-year-old man with a scar down one cheek, but an eight-year-old waif of a girl is a different story. He would make me scrub up and have my aunt plait my hair so I looked at least a little respectable, and then I would move among the gentry at Covent Garden or Bond Street, lifting purses and any other valuables I could get my hands on.'

His eyes narrowed as he thought of their first meeting on the bridge in St Ives. It seemed too much of a coincidence that he would accuse her of picking his pocket when she had spent her childhood doing just that.

'I have something important to ask you, Rose.'

She shifted in her seat, 'This is about when we met.'

He looked at her and then exclaimed, 'I knew it. I knew I felt your hand in my jacket.'

'I admit it,' she said after a moment, 'Although it was never my intention to steal anything.'

'What was your intention?'

She let out a long sigh. 'For the past two years I have had a stable home, somewhere I am happy and well paid. I am saving what money I can for my future, but I am all too aware how precarious my life is. I have no family, no one else to rely on except myself. Sometimes I panic.'

'And you try to pick a pocket?'

'I never actually steal anything,' she said with a vehement shake of her head. 'I wouldn't do that, not unless I was completely desperate, but I find it comforting to know that I still can.' She grimaced and took a sip of wine. 'Except it would seem I have lost my skills.'

'You pretend to pick pockets?'

'I slip my hand into someone's pocket and I see if I can lift out their purse. If my fingers close around it without them noticing, then I count it as a success. If not, then a fail. Until you I had not had many fails.'

'You are an unusual woman, Rose.'

'When you have known real hunger, the sort that comes from not having anything to eat for days on end, that deep gnawing in your belly, it changes you. Sometimes those changes lead to irrational ideas, but knowing I still have the skills from my childhood brings me some comfort, even though I hope I will never have to use them again.'

She smiled at him, but there was sadness there in her eyes and he had the urge to lean across the table and take her hands in his own. Quickly, he dismissed the thought, trying to bring the conversation back to safer ground.

'You mentioned your guardians—were they part of this criminal network?'

'No,' Rose said, some of the sadness lifting from her expression. 'Mr Wetherby caught me trying to steal from him one crisp winter's morning. He grabbed hold of my arm and I wasn't able to escape. Normally, I was quick, but it was frosty and I didn't have a coat, so my muscles were slow in the cold. He marched me away, ignoring my pleas, and I was sure I was about to be delivered to the magistrate. He'd caught me in the act and even though I was ten I knew there was a chance of transportation or perhaps even a death sentence. You can imagine how petrified I was. Instead of taking me to the magistrate, he took me home, to his warm kitchen and kindly wife.'

'They took you in?'

'Yes. They saw how thin I was, how close to starvation, how it was possible I might not survive a harsh winter. They offered me kindness and love and I knew from the very first moment I stepped inside their home that this was my chance to have a different life.'

'That was very generous of them, opening up their home to a stranger.'

'I asked my guardian about it before he became unwell and he said that he looked into my eyes when he caught me trying to pick his pocket and he saw a terrible desperation there. He thought he could do something about that.'

'They gave you the childhood you had never had.'

'They did. It took a while, but through patience and compassion they turned me from an angry, feral young girl into the person I am today.'

'You had never been to school before? Never learned to read or write?'

'No, but that was not something I struggled with too much. I wanted so desperately to read that I would stare at my letters at every free moment. When I eventually learned the basics, it was as though a whole new world opened up to me.'

'I am impressed,' Richard said and he meant it. Learning to read and write was a difficult enough skill to master if you did it at five or six years old, but leave it until a child was ten or eleven and it became infinitely harder.

'I owe the Wetherbys everything,' Rose said quietly.

'They have both passed now?'

'Yes, Mr Wetherby was quite advanced in years and he had an illness of the mind like your father. Mrs Wetherby outlived him by a few years, but she had a growth in her breast. I was working in Thetford at the time and she didn't tell me about it, didn't want to worry me.'

'You never got to say goodbye?'

'No. I wish I had been there with her at the end, to hold her like she had held me through those long nights when I had first gone to stay with the Wetherbys. She knew I loved her and that I was grateful for everything they had done for me, but I do wish I could have been there.'

'It sounds as though she was protecting you until the end.'

'Yes, I think you're probably right. She did want to protect me above all else.'

'I am glad you knew that, Rose, for a short while at least.' He closed his eyes for a moment, reflecting on how lucky he was in many ways. It was easy to get caught in the negative thoughts, to only think of the bad, but he had to remind himself other people had their hardships and their tragedies.

'Not many people had the childhood you did, Mr Digby,' she said softly, but there was a slight edge to her voice.

'I know.'

'It is worth remembering you are fortunate to have parents who loved you throughout everything that has occurred. Even though Lord Digby struggles to remember you now, he still loves you, your mother even more so.'

'I know.'

'She would be devastated if you left again, but she will never tell you herself.'

Richard fell silent. It was something he needed to talk to his mother about. He couldn't stay here, no matter how much his mother would want him to. It wouldn't be right, stepping into the role of Baron, taking the title, and living a life similar to the one Frederick Godrum should have had.

'You're planning on leaving, aren't you?'

'Yes. Eventually. I will stay while my father needs

me, while I can be of help to my mother, but once my father passes…' He trailed off.

'That could be a year or even more. Even the doctors have said things are unpredictable.'

'Then I shall be here for a year or more, but when it is over, I will leave.'

'What about the estate, your inheritance?'

'I will stay long enough to find a suitable steward, someone who can assist my mother while she still wishes to be involved and is primed to take over whenever she wants to step away from the duties of running the estate.'

'Perhaps do not tell your mother of your plans yet. It will devastate her.'

Rose picked up her glass and drained the last few drops of wine, placing it down firmly on the table once she had finished and bobbing into a formal little curtsy.

'Thank you for dinner,' she said, her tone suddenly clipped.

'You're leaving?'

'I need to go to bed in case your father wakes in the night.'

'Of course.'

Without another word, she spun around and walked from the room.

Richard sat back in his chair, wondering what specifically had upset her. She had changed when he had confirmed he would be leaving, but he wasn't sure if she was irritated that he would hurt his mother in such a way or sad he would be leaving because it would mean the end of their acquaintance.

For a long while he sat, spinning the wine glass in his hand, feeling as though he had made an almighty mistake this evening, but not sure which part the mistake had been.

Chapter Fifteen

Rose woke to the sun's rays falling on her face. It wasn't often she got to sleep past dawn and this morning she luxuriated in the indulgence of a few minutes in bed as she stretched and prepared for the day.

She had slept fitfully, her mind wanting to relive the kiss with Mr Digby again and again. Her waking moments had tangled with her dreams so that she had spent most of her night in a half-present daze, unsure what was real and what was not. It meant she had woken filled with regret and desire all bundled together.

'Damn you, Mr Digby,' she muttered as she rose from bed. He had burst into her peaceful life here at Meadow View and now she couldn't stop thinking about him.

Sitting on the edge of the bed, she told herself it was better than a different scenario. She could be living through a repeat of her last position with a manipulative master. This time she felt attraction towards Mr Digby, a strong pull that was hard to ignore. It was better than him pursuing her when she did not want anything to do with him and forcing her out of a good job.

At least they were both sensible people—one kiss need not ruin everything.

As she stood up, adjusting her nightdress so it sat straight on her shoulders, there was a frantic knocking on her bedroom door. She quickly put on her dressing gown and opened it to find Mr Watkins standing outside, panting heavily, his expression one of pure fear.

'He's gone,' he said through gasps.

Rose felt all the blood drain from her head and for a moment she swayed, having to reach out and hold on to the door to steady herself.

'What happened?'

'I woke half an hour ago and there was no sound coming from Lord Digby's bedroom. I got dressed as I normally do and then went in to check on him. He wasn't there. The bedclothes were tangled in a pile on the floor and his slippers gone, but there was no sign of him.'

'Where have you looked?'

'The front door is wide open, Miss Carpenter; he must have taken the key from the hook in the hall. I checked the glasshouse, but he is not in there.'

Rose felt panic rising within her as she remembered just a few days earlier when he had been heading straight for the river.

'Rouse everyone,' she said, already reaching for her dress. It was a blueish grey, still respectable and plain enough to be suitable as a maid's dress, but a little different to the other drab grey dresses she owned.

'Even Mr Digby?'

'No, I will knock on his door,' Rose said quickly. 'Set the footmen out to search the garden, starting with the land near the river. They can work their way back up towards the house. Mrs Green and the maids can search the house.'

Without another word, she closed the door on Mr Watkins and frantically began pulling off her dressing gown and nightdress. She was about to lift her nightdress over her head when the door to her room burst open and Mr Digby barrelled in.

The sight of her with her nightdress bunched at the level of her upper thighs made him stop suddenly, his eyes raking down her body as if she were completely naked and he could not help but stare.

'Forgive me,' he managed to bark out, turning abruptly so he was facing the other direction. 'I should not have burst in. I understand my father is missing.'

'Yes, Mr Watkins went to check on him and found he wasn't there. Mr Watkins is rousing the staff and they will have their orders on where to search.'

She stood there, nightdress still gripped in her hands, looking at Mr Digby's back. Her cheeks were burning, yet all she could think of was the elderly man who was probably distressed somewhere.

Still Mr Digby did not move and she was forced to take a step closer.

'I cannot join the search until I am dressed,' she said and finally he grunted in agreement and left her room.

She clicked the lock on her door this time, pulling her nightdress over her head before quickly donning the layers that made up her underclothes and dress.

Once dressed, she didn't waste any time trying to pin her hair, instead letting it fall loose about her shoulders. By the time she got downstairs, the servants had assembled and were all looking worried.

Lord Digby was well liked by his servants. The ones that had been there long enough to remember him from before his memory had started to wander could recall a kind and considerate master; those who had been there less time saw the infirm old man, but the patience and trust Lady Digby showed them was enough for them to know what Lord Digby would have once been like.

'Mrs Green, take the maids and search the house, top to bottom. Think of safe spaces, anywhere Lord Digby might crawl,' Rose said, taking charge from Mr Watkins. She felt a presence at her elbow as Mr Digby arrived. He gave her a nod to continue.

'The footmen are already off down the garden. As you suggested, they will start by the river and work up,' Mr Watkins said.

'Good. That leaves outside staff.' She turned to the stable boys and grooms who were looking excited at the prospect of adventure. 'Check all the outbuildings thoroughly. Mr Watkins, help them. Lord Digby will be disorientated and scared and might tuck himself away somewhere unexpected. Once you have finished there, we need to start searching the paths and roads that lead away from the house.'

'This has happened before, Miss Carpenter?' Mr Digby said as everyone hurried to their designated jobs.

'Yes. Your father likes to wander. We have held off locking his door at night—your mother thought it in-humane, but we may have to reconsider, at least while she isn't there sleeping in the bed beside him.'

'Do you ride, Miss Carpenter?'

'No.'

'Fine. I will saddle my horse and set off down the drive and then take the road in the direction of St Ives. Once the grooms are done, send one on horseback towards Hemingford Abbotts and the other to ride along the riverside path.'

She had expected him to be flustered, sharp with her even, but he was the picture of calm. She realised this was what he did, he swooped into perilous situations and contributed what he could.

'Thank you, Mr Digby.'

'You stay here and organise everyone, send out someone if my father is found before I return.'

'I will.'

Mr Digby left, walking from the hall without a backwards glance, heading towards the stables. Suddenly, Rose was all alone, the only sound coming from high above her as Mrs Green directed the maids where to start searching.

Rose paced backwards and forwards, wondering how far the old man could have got. She was surprised she hadn't heard him rise—normally, she was attuned to every sound that came from the room next to hers. Silently, she cursed Mr Digby for the kiss that had kept her tossing and turning into the early hours, even though she knew it was unfair to blame him for this.

It felt terrible not to be out there doing something. She wanted to be searching with everyone else, even though she knew Mr Digby was right to tell her to stay there. If someone came back with news of Lord Digby, or even with the old man himself, then there needed to be someone he trusted in the house to deal with whatever state he was in.

She bit at her thumbnail for a minute before letting out a growl of frustration. Biting her nails had been a habit of childhood, one she had long since stopped. Only in times of great pressure or worry did she find herself slipping back into the bad habit.

It seemed to take an age before the first of the searchers came trickling back, all eager to see if Lord Digby had been found elsewhere. The two footmen came first, having searched by the river and the garden, and with their return Rose felt her heart sink. Whenever Lord Digby had managed to wander off before he had always been found close to the house, normally somewhere in his beloved garden. It had been his pride and joy for years before his illness, and he seemed drawn to it now. It was not good news that he had not simply had the urge to smell the roses or meander among the summer flowers.

'I think you need to check along the river, go in either direction and scour the banks, make sure you check for any points where he could have slipped in,' Rose said, forcing the words out despite the lump in her throat. 'I will send one of the grooms on horseback once they have finished checking the stables and outbuildings.'

The footmen took off, long legs taking them quickly out of view round the side of the house. A few minutes later Rose sent the grooms off to saddle the horses and take the search out of the grounds of Meadow View.

'Nothing in the house, my dear,' Mrs Green said as she bustled into the hall. 'We've checked every nook and cranny and I don't think he's hiding anywhere in here.'

'You've checked under the beds?' Rose said, remembering the time Lord Digby had rolled beneath his impressive four-poster bed in a bid to feel safe when the confusion had taken over.

'Every bed.' Mrs Green came over to her and pulled Rose into her arms. 'You look terrible, my dear. We will find him, remember that. We've always found him before.'

Lord Digby going missing wasn't a new occurrence, but in the last few months they had become better at keeping him safely contained within the house and gardens without making it too obvious that he was trapped. It was the change in routine that had done it, with Lady Digby not being there. She should have asked Mr Watkins to take a small bed in the corner of Lord Digby's room while Lady Digby was away.

With a lurch, she thought of her mistress. Rose had sent her away to relax, to recuperate, but she would never forgive herself if it ended in tragedy.

'Stop,' Mrs Green said kindly. 'We will find him and get him home safe.'

Rose hoped desperately that the cook was right.

Richard felt his heart hammering in his chest as he reined in his horse to a gentle trot. His instinct was to fly down the lanes at speed, covering as much ground as possible, but he knew if he did that he was likely to miss something. His father might have climbed over a wall into a field or wandered off the road on any number of little tracks. If he sped through the lanes he would not see any potential clues that might alert him as to where his father had gone.

He wondered how far a frail old man could get in a few hours. They did not know what time he had left the house, but it must have been before six when the servants rose and began their work, otherwise surely they would have seen him wandering about. It meant he had been out and about for at least two hours.

A young, healthy man could cover a fair distance on foot in that time, but his father was slow and cautious when he walked, measuring out each step as if worried the ground might suddenly move beneath him. Surely he could not have got more than a couple of miles, perhaps even less given they thought he was wearing slippers on his feet.

Richard pulled gently on the reins as he thought he saw a flash of colour in the undergrowth to the side of the road, but it was just a patch of wildflowers and quickly he moved on.

It was as though he was living in a nightmare. All this time he had been away, leaving his mother to take responsibility for his father as well as the estate and all the work that came with having tenants and owning properties. She had managed admirably but had been close to exhaustion, so he had sent her away, yet it had only taken a few days until he had completely lost his father.

He thought of his conversation with Rose the night before. He had resolved to stay in England through the last months of his father's illness. Now Mr Godrum had passed away there was no threat to his freedom, no risk of being hauled in front of the magistrate and charged with partaking in an illegal duel.

He could stay in the country for as long as needed and that was what he meant to do. It was his responsibility, but more than that he wanted to be there. He wanted to ease the burden on his mother and do whatever he could to make the last months of his father's life as good as it possibly could be.

It would be difficult to leave after that, but somehow he would have to.

He had covered about a mile when he saw some grass flattened at the side of the road. It was subtle, but it looked as though something bigger than a dog had made its way through the long grass.

Dismounting, he took hold of the horse's reins and led him to the side of the road, peering into the undergrowth. There was a shallow ditch alongside the road with grass beyond it and a hedge separating the roadside from the meadow beyond. At the point where the grass was flattened there was also a small gap in the hedge, just big enough to squeeze through at a crouch.

Richard tied his horse to a tree a little further down the road and then made his way back to the flattened grass and the gap in the hedge.

'Hello?' he called softly. In all likelihood his father wasn't there, but if he was he didn't want to startle the old man by just appearing suddenly through the undergrowth.

There was no reply and Richard eyed up the ditch, deciding to jump over it and steady himself on the other side by clinging on to the hedge. When he had a stable footing, he bent low and half crawled, half scrambled into the meadow beyond.

At first glance the meadow was empty and, as Richard straightened and shielded his eyes from the sun, he felt a wave of disappointment. The flattened grass was most likely from some wild animal that had made its way through the hedge in the night. He was about to turn back to scramble through to the road when a small movement caught his eye.

He felt his hopes rise as he saw another movement in the long grass and cautiously started moving towards it.

Sitting hunched over at the edge of the meadow where it met the banks of the river was his father. Richard eyed the water only a few feet away nervously, remembering Rose's unfortunate dip a few days earlier. His father had been a strong swimmer once and Richard wondered if that sort of ability ever left you, but he wasn't keen to find out.

'Father.' He spoke softly, but he could tell by the slight tensing of the older man's shoulder that his father had heard him. 'It is Richard, I am here to take you home.'

He felt his heart squeeze as his father looked up at him with a flicker of clarity in his eyes.

'Richard?'

'Yes, Father. Everyone is worried about you.'

Lord Digby didn't move so Richard lowered himself to the ground beside him. As he looked sideways, he saw a tear roll down his father's cheek, glistening in the sunlight.

'I don't know what I am doing here,' Lord Digby said quietly. 'And I don't know how to get home.'

'It doesn't matter now,' Richard said, trying to disguise the emotion that threatened to spill out with every word he uttered. 'I can take you home.'

'Thank you,' Lord Digby said, but didn't move. Instead, the tears kept flowing down his cheeks as he let his body slump against Richard's.

For a long time, they sat there side by side. There was none of the agitation his father was normally plagued by, no demanding to see someone or do something. Instead, there was a quiet sadness about him. For a few moments at least it was as if he had remembered what he had lost and had a rare flicker of insight into his life now and what the future held.

'I don't think I ever told you how much I appreciated everything you did for me when I was young,' Richard said quietly. 'All those boys at school who talked about their terrible fathers, distant men, stern figures who only wished to see them once every few months to check they were not disgracing the family name. You were never like that.'

Richard paused and looked at his father. 'I know how lucky I was.' He fell silent, the words bubbling up inside him, but nothing he could say would be enough to express the gratitude he felt, so instead he wrapped his arm around his father's shoulders. 'I love you,' he said quietly.

'I love you, too, my boy.'

As the minutes ticked past, Richard spoke quietly to his father, reminiscing about happier times when he had been young. The carefree days before the duel when his life had been easy. He had fond memories of the summers they had spent exploring the waterways that stretched in all directions across Cambridgeshire, of hiking through the woods and setting up rudimentary camps when it got too late to travel back home.

After a while, his legs began to get stiff from sitting

on the hard earth and he was aware his father must be feeling it, too. It was impossible to know how long Lord Digby had been sitting there before Richard had come along, but he must be feeling the ache in his legs by now.

'Shall we go home, Father?' Richard said, standing and holding out a hand. He had to loop his hands under his father's arms to lift him to his feet and not for the first time he was struck by how thin his father had become under the nightshirt.

Lord Digby let Richard lead him across the uneven ground of the meadow and followed him through the gap in the hedge. He was limping a little and when Richard bent to inspect his feet there was a hole in one of the slippers and the skin had been rubbed raw as he walked.

'Let me help you on to the back of the horse,' Richard said, bracing himself as he half boosted, half lifted his father up into the saddle.

He took his time walking home, conscious of the people frantically searching for Lord Digby, but prioritising the frail old man who had not ridden in years. Thankfully, he did not slip from the saddle and Richard felt a great sense of relief as they turned into the drive of Meadow View.

As they approached the house, Rose came running out. Her eyes were red-rimmed and her cheeks flushed, but she was beaming now.

'You found him,' she said, running to his side. He got the impression she had nearly thrown her arms around him, but stopped herself just in time.

'He was sitting in a meadow a couple of miles away.'

'Is he hurt?'

'No. One of his feet has been rubbed raw, but apart from that I do not think he is injured.'

'I am so pleased you found him safe.' She turned her attention to Lord Digby. 'It is good to have you home, my lord.'

Lord Digby beamed at her, completely unaware of the panic he had caused.

'I shall send the stable boys out to find everyone who is searching,' Rose said over her shoulder as she took the old man's hand, leading him inside to safety.

Chapter Sixteen

Rose could not sleep. It had been a trying day and she felt terribly weary, but her mind was racing, and her senses heightened. Every little noise made her eyes jolt open, which made it impossible to sleep.

Lord Digby was relatively unharmed from his excursion out of the grounds of Meadow View. They had sent for the doctor, who had thoroughly checked him over and dressed the small wound on his foot. Doctor Griffiths had declared Lord Digby as well as could be expected and suggested he rest for a day in bed. This was impossible to achieve, of course, but the pain from his foot had limited his movement and he had stayed in his room for the rest of the day.

Earlier in the day, Mr Watkins had moved a small bed into the corner of Lord Digby's bedroom and tonight and every night from now on he would be there in case his master woke in the night. It should be reassuring, but Rose still felt shaken at how easily Lord Digby's early-morning wanderings could have turned into a disaster, so tonight she was attuned to every tiny noise.

She had spent the day looking after Lord Digby, but also doing her very best to avoid Mr Digby. Despite her resolve to try to forget the kiss they had shared she was finding it impossible. Every time he was close, she found herself drawn to him, listening intently to his every word and looking up at him as if he were the King himself. It irritated her, this reaction she had to him, and so she had resolved to avoid him.

Forcing herself to close her eyes and rest back on the pillow, she tried her very hardest to sleep. Just as she was about to drift off, a low moan roused her. She swung her legs out of bed immediately, taking her dressing gown from the hook behind her door and slipping it on as she quickly went into Lord Digby's room.

It took her eyes a moment to adjust to the darkness, but once they had she could see the figure of Lord Digby lying in the bed, sleeping peacefully. He was snoring slightly, just as he breathed in, his breath sometimes catching in his throat. On the small bed in the corner of the room Mr Watkins slept as well, but no noise came from him.

Wondering if she had imagined it, Rose left the room and closed the door behind her, stiffening as there was another cry, this time a little louder. Now she was up she could tell it hadn't come from Lord Digby's room, but from a little way along the upstairs hallway.

She hesitated. There was only one other person who slept here on the first floor and that was Mr Digby. She was hardly going to burst into his room because he was talking in his sleep, but still it felt strange to leave a man shouting out.

Everything was quiet as she crept along the hall and

by the time Rose got to Mr Digby's door she felt foolish, glad there was no one to see her creeping along in
the darkness. She was about to head back to bed when
there was another low moan, followed by a thrashing
and then a series of increasingly agitated shouts. Rose
waited, hoping the shouts would calm as they had before or that Mr Digby would wake himself if his thrashing got too violent, but it didn't happen. Instead, he was
getting louder and louder.

Rose checked back over her shoulder. She hated to
hear anyone in such distress, but she was also aware that
Lord Digby's room wasn't too far away. If the commo-
tion continued much longer it might wake the old man
and then he would be impossible to settle.

Before she could talk herself out of it, she knocked
on Mr Digby's door, waiting for a moment and then
trying the handle.

It was a little lighter in the room than the hallway,
the curtains letting in some of the silvery moonlight.
Immediately, she could see Mr Digby's dark form in
the bed, tossing and turning.

'Mr Digby,' she called, not wanting to go fully inside.

He did not stir and now the shouts were getting increasingly frenzied. His words were incoherent, but a
few times she heard *stop* and wondered if he was reliving the moment Frederick Godrum turned the pistol
up to his face and peered down the barrel the moment
before the shot released.

'Mr Digby,' she said again, stepping into the room
now. She walked slowly, aware it would be a huge shock
for him to find her here when he did wake up.

Still he did not stir. Rose was almost at the bed now

and could make out the outline of his body. She was shocked to find his torso exposed and bare and for a few seconds her eyes lingered. Deep inside her she felt a longing that she had never felt before and had the urge to slip into bed beside him and press her body against his.

Forcing her eyes away, she reprimanded herself. She was meant to be here to help him, nothing more. She reminded herself of the horror in his eyes after the kiss that they had shared and the promise she had made to herself after the disastrous affair with Mr Rampton to only give away her heart to someone who could love her back fully without restrictions. Mr Digby was not that man.

She crouched down beside him and reached out, taking his hand that hung over the side of the bed. There was a pause in the moans coming from him as her hand gripped his, but after a second he began to toss again.

'Mr Digby,' she whispered, gripping his hand tighter. 'You're shouting in your sleep.'

For a moment, his eyes flickered open, but Rose could see he was not properly awake as they did not focus on her. He gripped her hand tighter, pulling her in closer so that now Rose's face was just a few inches from his own.

Despite not waking properly, Mr Digby seemed to settle a little. His shouts turned to murmurs and although there was still a panicked quality to them it wasn't the outright fear he had displayed before.

Rose squeezed his hand again, torn between trying to extricate herself now he had calmed and wanting to ensure he was fully settled before she crept from the room. In response, he gripped her even tighter. Panicked, Rose wiggled, realising that he was holding her so firmly she could not slip her hand from his.

She didn't want him to wake, to see her there crouching by the side of his bed. Not now his nightmare was passing and there was no good reason for her to be there. After ten seconds of trying to manoeuvre her hand free unsuccessfully, she stood up, thinking to use height as leverage. At the same moment, Mr Digby's eyes shot open and he let out a low, primal growl.

Rose felt him tug on her arm, still not releasing her hand, and she couldn't help but tumble forward, her body moving towards his at speed. Within a second her abdomen had hit his bare chest and the momentum meant she half fell, half rolled over him, ending up lying on her back in his bed.

Before she had chance to work out what had just happened, Mr Digby had flipped himself over and was using his body to pin her to the bed. They were both breathing hard and Rose had to bite back a scream. It had all happened so fast—one second, she was trying to pull her hand from his, the next, he had flipped her into his bed and pinned her there with his body.

She could see his disorientation as his eyes searched her face and it took a few seconds for him to realise it was her trapped underneath him and not a stranger.

'Rose,' he said, his voice still heavy with sleep. 'What are you doing?'

It was an impossible question to answer in just a few words and with her heart hammering in her chest and her breathing coming fast and hard she couldn't bring herself to say anything at all.

As she lay there, wrists pinned to the bed by Mr

Digby's strong hands, she was acutely conscious of his body pressed against hers. His lower half was wrapped in a thin sheet and she wore her nightdress, but the layers were thin and Rose could feel the heat of his body against hers.

For a long moment his eyes searched hers and she could see confusion and longing all mixed together.

'What are you doing here, Rose?' He sounded a little more awake this time, but still he made no move to roll off her.

'You were shouting,' she said, her voice catching in her throat. 'I was worried you might wake Lord Digby, so I came and knocked on your door, but you carried on shouting.'

'So, you came in?'

Now she was having to say the words out loud it sounded a foolish idea. Maids would often think nothing of entering their masters' and mistress' rooms while they were sleeping, creeping in to lay a fire or fetch some clothes that needed to be washed first thing in the morning, but it was very different to entering in the middle of the night.

'I'm sorry,' she said, unable to tear her eyes away from his. There was a burning intensity there and Rose felt his body shift slightly above her. It sent a pulse of longing through her and for a moment she had the urge to reach up, loop an arm round his neck and pull his lips to hers and damn the consequences.

She watched as his eyes flicked to her lips and wondered if he was thinking the same thing.

'You were shouting. I couldn't leave you.'

Another five seconds passed, then ten, and then

eventually he let out a tortured groan and rolled away from her, taking the sheet, and wrapping it round his lower body as he stood. Rose's eyes widened as she realised, he must be naked underneath the thin layer.

'I am sorry my nightmares disturbed you,' he said from a safe distance of a few feet away.

Rose scrambled up on to her elbows, aware she was now sprawled in his bed. Her cheeks were burning and her thoughts jumbled and it was all made worse when in her haste one of her arms buckled and she was sent sprawling back into his pillows. She caught a hint of his scent and the desire she had desperately been trying to suppress came flooding back.

'Are you planning on staying in my bed?' Mr Digby asked, raising an eyebrow. She could tell it was meant to be a comment to lighten the mood, but his voice came out low and seductive.

Rose forced herself to breathe evenly, refusing to scrabble out of the bed and run from the room. Instead, with as much dignity as she could muster, she shuffled to the edge and stood up.

'I apologise for disturbing your sleep,' she said formally, holding her head high as she began to walk away.

She had only taken two steps when Mr Digby reached out and gripped her wrist, his fingers warm on her skin.

'Forgive me,' he said quietly. 'I was shocked, that is all. A man does not expect to wake up to find an attractive woman next to his bed. I was thrown, but my reaction was not acceptable. Thank you for waking me from the nightmare.'

Rose nodded. She wanted to ask him about the dream, to see if it was as she thought, a reliving of the tragic day eight years earlier when he had witnessed his friend's death. She almost did, almost opened her mouth to speak, but instead she gave one final nod and hurried from the room.

Outside, she let out a sigh of relief. It had been too dangerous standing in the bedroom with Mr Digby. All she could think of was how it felt with his body pressed against hers, his hands pinning her to the bed, his lips only inches away from making her forget every reason they could not share even one more kiss. Her body felt weak and spent, as if she had run miles over difficult terrain, and her legs wobbled as she hurried back to her room.

Inside, she scrambled into bed and pulled the bedcover up high, pulling them tightly around her body. She was struggling to remember why it was a bad idea to kiss the man she felt such desire for, and when she closed her eyes, she could almost imagine he was climbing into bed beside her.

'He can't give you what you need,' she whispered in the silence. Even if he let himself enjoy a few weeks of guilt-free pleasure, it was certainly not what Rose needed. She needed someone who was free to love her, to cherish her, to want to build a future. She wanted something wholesome and lasting, not a quick fling from which he would walk away with his reputation intact and she would face ruin once again and probably lose her position.

Flipping over, she buried her face in the pillow and

let out a muted scream, nothing loud enough to wake Lord Digby in the next room, but good for venting some of her frustrations with the world.

Chapter Seventeen

'We have three more days,' Mr Digby said as he passed her in the hall.

She was on her way to the servants' stairs with a heavy basin of water, her arms straining under the load. She had taken it up to allow Mr Watkins to shave Lord Digby, but the elderly man had refused vehemently and so the basin of water was untouched and full almost to the brim.

'Three more days until what?'

'Until Lady Digby returns home. She is staying with my aunt until Saturday and then will return home that evening. The journey is not arduous and should only take her a couple of hours.' He brandished a letter that must have been delivered by a messenger that morning.

'Good,' Rose said, her voice a little strained from the effort of keeping the bowl steady and level. 'I hope she has had a good rest.'

'Yes. She always used to like visiting my aunt so I am hopeful it will have been restorative for her.'

Rose nodded, but didn't answer, keen to get the heavy

bowl back down the stairs before her arm muscles became strained.

Richard looked at her curiously. 'I think we probably need to talk about last night.'

Rose had barely slept. Each time she had closed her eyes she had been transported back to his bed, pinned underneath him, desperate for him to kiss her. She had risen this morning tired and grumpy and right now she had a hundred things to do before lunch.

'Perhaps not right this instant,' she said, flicking her eyes down to the bowl. It was an excuse, but a helpful one. She had lain awake until the sun had started to rise that morning, listening to the birds and trying to suppress the feeling of melancholy that had descended upon her.

After their encounter in Mr Digby's bed the night before, Rose had allowed herself to admit she felt something for the man. She didn't want to examine too closely what that something was, but she could not deny the way her body had responded to him.

It was an uncomfortable realisation, but more than that it made her sad. Nothing could ever happen between them, nothing meaningful or lasting. Even the idea of friendship was laughable when she truly thought about it. He was a man of a very different social status to hers.

'Ah, of course. Let me take it for you.' He stepped closer, reaching out his hands.

'You do not need to take it, I can manage the bowl,' she snapped, her tone a little sharper than she had meant it to be. Never before had she minded being a servant. She mostly enjoyed her work and was grateful for the opportunities she had received to pull herself from the gutter, but today she wished she was something more, that she held a position that meant a kiss between her and Mr Digby wasn't such a scandalous disaster.

'Give me the bowl, Rose, it is no trouble to take it downstairs.' He reached out further, his fingers looping around the ceramic of the bowl and brushing against hers.

'No. I can carry a bowl of water downstairs. I have been doing it for years. I have not suddenly become incapable.'

He didn't drop his hands and, as she looked at him, she could tell he thought she was being unreasonable. She *was* being unreasonable. He was offering to help, but every time he reached out it reminded her that it was her job to serve his family, to carry their bowls of water and clean their clothes. It shone a light on the great chasm between them and she was finding it hard to control herself so he wouldn't see how much that devastated her.

'Do not martyr yourself, Rose. The bowl is heavy, you are finding it a strain, let me take it.'

'No,' she said, louder than she meant to. She wrenched her hands back, pulling the bowl with her, at the same time as Mr Digby let go. She spluttered as the lukewarm water tipped and splashed out of the bowl all over her face and chest.

In shock, she took a couple of staggering steps backwards and then stared at the huge puddle of water on the floor.

'Rose...' Mr Digby said.

She held up a hand. 'Please do not say another word.'

'You're being unreasonable.'

She felt an explosion of rage and sorrow fly through her and come bursting out, and in the instant before she began speaking, she thought she saw Mr Digby's eyes widen.

'Unreasonable?' she asked, but didn't give him time to answer. 'Shall I tell you what is unreasonable? Unreasonable is engaging a maid in conversation when she is clearly carrying a heavy bowl that needs to be taken down a steep flight of stairs and be disposed of in the kitchen.' She shook her head and flicked some of the excess water from her skin. 'Unreasonable is thinking that everyone should fall in line whenever you suggest something, even if you are not the right person to make the rules. Unreasonable is—'

'Rose,' Mr Digby interrupted her. 'Breathe.'

She glanced up at him and for a moment her voice caught in her throat. She wanted to throw herself into his arms and take the comfort he was offering, but that would only make matters worse. Instead, she resolved to push him away in the only way she knew how, even if the words ended up hurting her as much as they did him.

'Do not tell me to breathe. You have absolutely no idea what is needed to be done in the next couple of hours, so the day runs smoothly for your father, no idea how much work I have to squeeze into my day. Why should you? I am a mere servant, a maid, nothing more. Of course, you think it is your right to stop me in the middle of a task to make small talk,' she scoffed and shook her head, some of her anger dissipating as the water dripped off her on to the floor. 'Of course, it *is* your right,' she muttered, feeling her cheeks flush.

'Rose, I am sorry,' he said, but she could tell he wasn't certain what he was apologising for.

She felt terrible, lashing out, and it had only made things worse. She wanted to reach out and explain, to show him that it was her sorrow for what could never be and the reminder of her inferior place in the world that had made her speak so harshly, but she couldn't find the words.

'It doesn't matter,' she said abruptly and turned away, hoping he wouldn't see the tears in her eyes, quickly heading for the servants' stairs. 'Don't slip in that water.'

Richard stared after her, unsure whether to follow her and try to understand what her outburst had really been about or whether to give her a few minutes to calm down. He decided on the latter. They needed to talk, but he would get nowhere while she was spitting fire.

He popped in to see his father and found him in a combative mood, grouchy after a few days where his routine had been changed and from the tiredness that had come after the long walk he had taken yesterday morning.

'I will try to get him to have a rest later this morning, sir,' Mr Watkins said quietly as he sat with Lord Digby, 'But he has been unpredictable so far today, so I cannot promise anything.'

Taking a seat at the piano, Richard let his fingers drift over the keys. His father had found the music relaxing earlier in the week and he hoped it might have the same effect today. Richard needed it, too. The pieces he could play on the piano were imprinted in his memory and it took very little to remember how to move his fingers across the keys. It meant playing the piano was wonderfully relaxing and he felt as though he needed something to occupy him so his thoughts could wander.

Once he was certain his father was enjoying the slow, haunting melody, he picked out on the keys, Richard allowed himself to think of Rose. She had not reappeared yet, no doubt mopping up the spilled water in the hall and changing her soaking dress.

He suspected her reaction today was related to how he had reacted last night when he woke to find her in his room. In the darkness he had panicked, unable to see at first who it was crouching there beside him. His first thought had been self-defence and he'd flipped her on to the bed and pinned her down.

He stumbled over a note as he remembered the way her body had felt beneath him. She was petite, but the shapeless nightgown hid her curves. As he had sat atop her, holding her wrists above her head, he'd desperately had to fight the urge to lower himself over her and claim her as his own.

He could tell the attraction was not just on his part. Last night as she lay underneath him he had felt the subtle press of her hips into his and seen the way her cheeks had flushed as their eyes had locked. Rose might be acting distant today, but perhaps that was because she had felt that irresistible desire the night before and it had scared her. Or perhaps she was still annoyed at him for some other unspoken crime.

It was impossible to know which, and as he sat playing the piano, he decided he would somehow find out. He couldn't ignore the simmering attraction between them, but he also didn't want to frighten Rose away.

She was kind and patient with his father and without a doubt made his life better than it would be without her there. The last thing he wanted was to make it uncomfortable for her here in her own home.

The door opened and Rose entered, looking more composed than she had earlier. Richard regarded her out of the corner of his eye, seeing that she was fastidiously avoiding looking at him.

After a few more pieces, he stood and approached his father, who as now dozing quietly in the chair.

'Let me know if he is still agitated when he wakes,' he said to Mr Watkins. 'I need to speak to Miss Carpenter, but once she is back, I suggest you have a rest. I am aware you cannot have slept very well, keeping one ear out for my father.'

'Thank you, sir. That is kind of you to think of me.'

As time passed, he was getting into the routine of the household a little, gradually seeing how things worked. It was what he had done in the Dutch East Indies and some of the other places he had stayed: taken his time to assess the situation, see whether he could be of help without being a burden on stretched resources. Only once he had spent some time ascertaining these things did he step forward and see what he could offer.

Now he thought he could see a little more clearly how things worked at Meadow View. His mother was right, Rose was an angel where his father was concerned. She was patient and kind and gentle, but she didn't mind getting her hands dirty. She was the perfect combination of maid and companion.

Mr Watkins was also a great asset to the household here at Meadow View. He was quieter than Rose, slightly more deferential when he spoke to Lord Digby, but this all would help the older man feel as though he were just a normal valet, rather than a caretaker.

They were lucky, although he was aware it was more than pure luck. His mother had no doubt scoured the local area to find the best-suited people to make a harmonious and happy household that was capable of safely looking after Lord Digby.

The slight flaw in the set-up that he could see was the fact that out of necessity his father was sometimes left alone and this meant he was liable to wander. All the disasters with his father while he had been home had been due to the older man wandering off where he was not supposed to, but he was aware there was a balance to be had. They couldn't confine him to his rooms, lock him up like a caged animal. They had to balance his safety with his freedom and happiness.

It was a problem he would puzzle over.

'Miss Carpenter, while my father sleeps there are one of two things we need to discuss. Once we have done so I suggest you relieve Mr Watkins so he can rest for a while.'

'Of course, Mr Digby,' she said, her tone neutral and her features fixed into a bland expression.

He left the room first, not turning to check if Rose was following behind him. Downstairs, he eschewed the option of the study, instead leading the way out into the garden. It was another beautiful day with the sun shining and only a few wispy clouds high in the sky. Later, it would be hot, but for now it was the perfect temperature for a stroll.

'I think we need privacy for this,' he said, eyeing the

gardeners who were working hard on trimming any dead heads off the roses and other early-summer flowers.

'I cannot be away long, sir,' Rose said formally. He ignored her comment and led the way across the lawn, turning left at the bottom before they reached the river. There was a secluded part of the garden, still within the boundaries of Meadow View, but left to grow wild like the meadows beyond. At one end of this his father had put a bench overlooking the flowers and the water, ideal for whiling away the hours on a beautiful summer's day, or for a private talk when the subject was going to be difficult.

'Shall we sit here? I do not think we will be overheard.'

'Only by the bees and the beetles,' Rose murmured.

She sat down at one end of the bench, leaving as much gap between them as possible.

'I am sorry for what happened this morning,' he said, thinking starting with an apology might appease some of the fury he had seen earlier and allow them to talk through the actual issue.

'Why are you sorry?' she said, turning to him with anger in her eyes.

This surprised him and he hesitated for a moment.

'An apology means nothing if you do not know what you are apologising for.'

'Rose,' he said, a note of warning in his voice. A lot had happened between them, but he wasn't going to just allow her to berate him without any response.

She pressed her lips together, making two tiny dimples appear in her cheeks.

'I am sorry I did not think how heavy that basin of

water must have been to hold and I am sorry I reached out for it without asking you if you wanted me to,' he said eventually. 'But I don't think this is about a basin of water.'

For a long moment she stared into the distance. 'Do you know how many orders I have been given in my life? Fetch this, carry that, make this bed, clean up that mess.' She shook her head.

'You don't like me giving you orders.'

'I have no problem with you giving me orders. I work for you, or at least I work for your mother. I even quite like my job and I like doing it well.'

Richard sat back, completely lost. He waited as Rose's eyes flicked backwards and forward between two spots on the horizon.

'When I worked for Mr Rampton, he loved to order me around. He would use his power over me and got some sort of horrible thrill from it. It became part of our interactions nearly every day. He would do something like summon his children to recite their letters or numbers to him and orchestrate it so they would knock over a glass. The children would be sent away and he would order me to clear up after them.'

She glanced at him and gave a wry smile. 'You're thinking that was my job, to clear up after the children.' Her voice was flat and there was very little emotion in her voice, as if she had blocked out much of what had happened to her.

'I understand there are ways of asking people to do things.'

'He wouldn't ask, he would gesture and then he would stand over me while I cleaned up whatever mess it was. He would just tower over me with his arms crossed and this little smile on his face.'

'This was when you were…intimate?' He hated the idea of a man taking advantage of Rose, of pressuring her until he found a weak moment when she just folded and gave in.

'Before that even, but I think it was worse after. It was obvious he liked the power imbalance between us. He oversaw every part of my life and he loved to remind me that nothing was my own.'

'He sounds a scoundrel.'

'He was,' Rose said, shaking her head. 'Sometimes I look back and I feel such self-loathing that I ever let myself be dragged into his world and I hate that I stayed for so long. I knew what he was doing to me, knew how he was trying to make me feel worthless, but still I stayed.'

Richard shifted, turning towards her. He couldn't quite link what had happened this morning to her scoundrel of an old employer.

'You are nothing like Mr Rampton,' Rose said softly. 'Absolutely nothing like him, yet this morning I realised I would always be just a servant to you.'

Richard frowned, now totally lost, and Rose gave a long-suffering sigh. When she spoke again the words tumbled out quickly and he had to listen carefully to keep up.

'I know nothing can happen between us, I know that kiss we shared can never be repeated, I know you are not looking for or wanting a relationship in any form. I don't want one either. Yet it would be nice to have the option. Instead, I will always be a servant to you.' She glanced at him and must have seen his troubled expression for she pushed on quickly.

'If I was a young woman of your social class there wouldn't have been any question of me carrying that basin of water, yet until I drew your attention to it you didn't even notice I was struggling. You will never notice, for I am a servant and in your mind a servant carrying a heavy bowl of water is nothing unusual.'

'You're upset about the difference in our social status?' Richard said. 'Even though you do not want a relationship with me nor I you.'

Rose buried her head in her hands and Richard reached out instinctively, placing a hand on her leg just above the knee. He felt her stiffen at the contact, but she did not push him away.

'I don't want to want you,' she murmured. 'I don't want to want to kiss you. I am all too aware that if we did kiss again nothing would come of it because we were born into different circumstances.'

'If you don't want anything to happen between us, does it matter?'

'Yes,' she answered, almost growling the words. 'What I want is to fall in love with a nice young man who would not be ashamed to court me. Perhaps someone with a trade or a shopkeeper, someone who knows the value of hard work. I want to find someone I will be equal with, someone who cannot stand over me and point to the ground and watch me as I scrub and clean.

'Yet instead I find myself once again entangled with a man who could have me dismissed from my position with a click of his fingers, who could order me to clean every pot and pan in the house and then once they were clean order me to do them again.' She looked at him, her eyes beseeching, and he saw how much she was hurting. 'I know nothing more will happen between us, but I do not even want to feel this…turmoil inside.'

'Rose, do you know what I see when I look at you?'

She shook her head.

'I see a beautiful young woman who is not afraid to speak her mind, someone who cares for my father as if he were her own.'

'I am not asking you to forget I am a servant. I know that is not possible.' She dropped her head again and pressed her lips together, searching for the words before continuing. When she looked up at him her eyes were wet with tears.

'I find myself wishing I had never met you. These last two years I have tried my hardest to build my confidence and my belief that the next time I would make the right decision, then one look from you and I am making the same mistakes all over again.'

'Not the same mistakes, Rose.'

'Not the same, but similar enough that I should know better. You are not a controlling or cruel, but there is a difference in social status between us and I am the one at a disadvantage.'

Richard nodded silently, taking in everything she had said. He could understand what she was saying, understand the hurt she was still suffering for the time she had lost giving in to Mr Rampton's demands. He could even see how the difference in their statuses would make her uncomfortable.

It made him uncomfortable when he stopped and thought about it, but if there was to be nothing more between them, if all it ever amounted to was a kiss and a lot of pent-up desire, then surely the gulf between them did not matter so much.

'One day you will find your nice young man, Rose. A man who treats you with all the respect you deserve and surrounds you with love.' Even as he said the words he felt a pang of jealousy. For a moment he could imagine her walking hand in hand with a handsome, hearty man, with a gaggle of children running just in front.

The vision made his heart squeeze in his chest and he realised that, although he would never begrudge her happiness, he did not want to think of her with someone else.

'You forget where I come from,' she said quietly. 'Perhaps I don't believe in happy endings. I saw few enough of them growing up.'

He felt a surge of sympathy for the young woman. She had overcome so much in her life, he didn't like to see her unhappy now.

Rose swallowed hard and tried to regain her composure. She had never meant to let slip the terrible turmoil she was feeling. It wasn't something Mr Digby needed to know about, yet there was something about him when he leaned in close and looked at her as though she was the only woman in the world. Then her tongue loosened and her secrets slipped out.

She felt her cheeks flush as she realised she had told him of the desire she felt for him. Mr Digby was not stupid, he would have known from the way she reacted to his touch that she was attracted to him, but there was a certain protection afforded by being able to deny it.

She had dashed that and told him she desired him and now there was nowhere to hide.

Looking down, she realised his hand was still on her leg, resting on the material of her dress, his fingers moving just a fraction every now and then as he shifted next to her.

'You shouldn't touch me,' she said quietly.

They both looked down to where his hand rested, staring at the fingers outlined against the blue-grey of her dress.

'No,' he said. 'I shouldn't.' For a long moment he sat there unmoving. 'I feel it too, Rose. That push and pull of desire and regret. It is not just you.' It seemed hard for him to admit, and Rose realised he was not used to talking about his feelings.

His strategy the last eight years had been to bottle everything up and push it deep down inside him. It was a terrible way to deal with things and one day everything would come bubbling out. Yet Rose could not see him changing anytime soon.

As she looked up into his eyes, she felt a flare of rebellion inside her. She wanted to smash through all the rules and the standards, she wanted to rail against how unfair it was to put people into little boxes and not ever let them rise. Nothing could make a liaison between her and Mr Digby appropriate and it made her want it even more.

Before she could fully understand what she was doing, she leaned over and kissed Mr Digby on the lips. At first it was a gentle kiss, nothing more than her lips brushing ever so softly against his. Then as the fire rose inside her she deepened it, twisting her body and pulling him closer, feeling a perverse pleasure at all the rules they were breaking.

For one minute she wanted to forget she was a maid, forget that society would do their very best to keep her mixing only with her own kind. She pushed away the very reason she had been angry in the first place and tried to forget how the man she was kissing had the power to ruin her life.

At first Mr Digby's lips were unyielding as he tried to resist the wave of desire she knew he was feeling, but after a few seconds he let out a low groan and kissed her back. He was less gentle this time, more insistent, looping his arm around her and swinging her on to his lap so her body was pressed against his.

She knew it could not last long. Soon one of them would have to be the sensible one and break off the kiss, but she was determined to enjoy every second that it lasted.

Eventually, they pulled apart, both a little dazed.

'Rose...'

She smiled at him and pressed a finger to his lips.

'I know,' she said, shaking her head sadly. 'That shouldn't have happened.'

'No, it shouldn't.'

She was still sitting on his lap, straddling his legs, her skirt stretched out and hitched up, and she could tell he was reluctant to let her go despite his words.

'And it can't happen again,' she said, leaning in closer so her lips were only a hair's breadth from his.

'It can't happen again.'

For a long moment they stayed like that, lips almost touching, her chest rising and falling in time with his.

Eventually, Mr Digby let out a growl of frustration and stood, picking her up with him before setting her feet on the ground. Only then did he break away from her, walking a few steps away, his face turned away.

Rose closed her eyes and took a few deep breaths. The kiss had been foolish and something that would not be repeated, no matter how much she yearned to be back in Mr Digby's arms. She would listen to the rational part of her mind and remember she deserved to be with someone who could love her, someone who wasn't stuck in the past and someone who could walk down the road hand in hand with her without the whole world staring and whispering.

'I think I should return to the house,' Rose said.

Mr Digby was still turned away so she couldn't see his expression and he didn't answer. She waited for a moment and then smoothed down her skirts before walking briskly back in the direction of the house.

Chapter Eighteen

Richard felt as though he had been punched in the gut and even now a few minutes later hadn't got his breath back properly.

'Damn you, Rose,' he muttered.

It had been the most confusing ten minutes of his life. First, she had acted aloof, annoyed with him for first not taking the basin of water and then annoyed when he had tried to. Then she had told him a little about how her last employer had abused his position of power over her and how she still regretted letting him have that hold on her for so long.

Finally, she had lamented their differences in social status before kissing him. The kiss had been the most un-expected part. She had not been happy with him through-out the whole preceding conversation, then suddenly she had kissed him.

Now she had disappeared back to the house, leaving him feeling frustrated with pent-up desire and completely confused about what it was she wanted.

'I'm not interrupting anything, am I?' Sebastian

called as he climbed over the stile that separated the grounds of Meadow View from the fields beyond. The lively dog that had accompanied him a few days earlier trotted at his heels, barking happily as he spotted someone new to play with.

Richard's eyes narrowed as he calculated the direction Sebastian would have come from, wondering how much he had seen between Richard and Rose.

'No,' he said, a little more abruptly than he meant to.

Thankfully, Sebastian either didn't notice his tone or ignored it. 'Another glorious day. Was that Miss Carpenter I saw leaving as I came round the bend in the river?'

'Yes. We were discussing my father's care.'

'Ah, I see.'

'How does Elizabeth fare?'

'Better each day. She is out of bed now and Dr Griffiths says she will be back to normal activities within the week.'

'I am glad.'

'How is your father?'

Richard grimaced and told his friend of the disaster the day before when his father had gone for his early morning wander.

'It means we are having to keep an even closer guard on my father, which of course he will not like.'

'No, no man likes to feel his movements are restricted and his freedom limited.' Sebastian looked at him for a long moment as if deciding whether to say any more. 'How are you faring, Digby? It must be a shock to be home, to come back to everything you left behind after so long.'

'It is. I feel unsettled, restless.'

'You want to leave?'

Richard considered the question and realised with surprise that the answer was no, despite the terrible situation with his father, despite the gnawing guilt he felt at being back in the country when he had vowed never to return. He felt on edge much of the time, eager to spring into action, but he didn't actually want to leave.

He enjoyed being with his father and the sense of worth it gave him when he contributed to the older man's care. He enjoyed being back in the place of his childhood, even if the memories were tinged with darkness. For an instant his mind flicked to Rose and he had to acknowledge he enjoyed her company, too, even if this was something he should not allow himself.

'No, not yet at least.'

'Good.'

'I will stay while my father needs me. I think it will be a difficult few months.'

'And then?'

'Then I leave.'

Sebastian blew out his cheeks and exhaled softly as if trying to find the best way to approach a delicate subject. 'Amelia holds no animosity towards you, Digby.'

'She told me.'

'She cares for you like I do.'

'She is quite the most generous woman I have ever met.'

'She does not wish for you to go on punishing yourself.'

Richard glanced up at his friend and shook his head, but couldn't find the words to speak.

'That is what you are doing with this self-imposed exile. You are keeping yourself away from the things that could make you happy: your family, a home, a future with a wife and children.'

Still, Richard didn't say anything, knowing his friend was partially right, but also aware he could never grasp the intricacies of the situation.

'You cannot punish yourself for ever, Digby. You made a mistake, one that ended with a man losing his life, but you did not kill him—hell, you did not even challenge him to a duel.'

'I did accept, though; I did go along and pick up my pistol from its case.'

'As any of us would have done at that age. You were barely into adulthood. You cannot let this one mistake rule your whole life.'

Richard sighed and closed his eyes. It was not the first time he had heard this argument and often he wished it were true, but the truth was it *did* rule his life. It was a terrible act that would plague him until the day he died.

'I am not suggesting you forget Godrum, but I think you need to work on forgiving yourself, otherwise it is as if you died alongside Godrum eight years ago.'

'A man died because of me, Sebastian. If I had acted differently, he would be alive. Perhaps I should be punished my whole life. Why should I get to have a home, a family, an idyllic life when he does not?'

'You did not kill him.' Sebastian held up a hand and gave Richard a smile. 'I do not wish to berate you, it is just I hate to see you wasting your life, hating yourself. I want you to feel a little bit of happiness at least.'

Richard felt the last of his friend's words strike him in the chest. Happiness seemed a foreign concept, something that had once been part of his life, but was now a wispy memory. As he had the thought, he realised it wasn't quite true. These last few days he had felt flashes of it, fleeting and brief, but happiness all the same, when he was with Rose. She made him smile and for a few moments she made him forget.

He frowned, aware that forgetting was no good thing, but it was true. When he was with Rose, he found some of the heaviness on his shoulders lifted and his smile came a little quicker.

'Perhaps there is someone who makes you feel happy,' Sebastian said with a forced nonchalance.

Richard's head whipped round, but his friend's eyes were fixed on a point in the distance.

'If there is, it wouldn't be a bad thing to grab hold of that happiness, even if it isn't the most conventional of relationships.'

'You saw,' Richard said flatly.

'Yes, didn't mean to spy, but it was difficult not to see.'

'It is impossible, a mistake.'

'It didn't look like a mistake.'

Richard's eyes widened and he looked at his friend. 'She is a maid, Sebastian.'

Sebastian shrugged. 'Certainly not the choice most of society would make for you, but what does it truly matter? I do not think that is your real reason for holding back, is it?'

'Perhaps not, but nothing more is going to happen.'

'She is a lovely girl. Very clever and compassionate.'

'I cannot believe the Earl of Cambridgeshire is trying to set me up with a housemaid.'

Sebastian sighed. 'Would I feel a little easier if she was the daughter of some titled gentleman? Yes, of course, but I caught the expression on your face when you looked at her. I think for the first time in years she has woken you from the numbness of your existence. She has sparked a feeling inside you that is something other than self-loathing and regret. She might not be the woman you marry, but there are many types of relationships in this world.'

Richard bristled, thinking of Rose's torment under her last employer.

'It is not going to happen,' he said abruptly.

'She's a pretty girl, and by the way she was looking at you, I would say she's fallen for you.'

'It's not going to happen,' Richard said again, even firmer this time.

'I doubt she is an innocent…she may even welcome the suggestion she become your mistress.'

Richard spun quickly, feeling a flash of anger like nothing he had ever felt before. He stepped closer to Sebastian, but caught himself before he could lash out. These last eight years he had mastered his self-control, but a few words about Rose and Sebastian was testing his limits.

'Do not talk of Miss Carpenter in that way,' he said through clenched teeth.

Sebastian held up his hands, looking at Richard curiously. 'I apologise. I did not mean to cause offence. I hold Miss Carpenter in high regard and do not mean to insult her, I only thought to show you that there are ways you can be together.' He paused as the little dog jumped up at him, yapping at his knees. 'She means something to you, then?'

Richard remained silent. He wasn't ready to think about why he felt so protective of Rose Carpenter. He wanted to tell Sebastian of what she had been through, what she had suffered to get to where she was, then perhaps the man would see she was so much more than a servant, but it wasn't his story to tell. There was no doubt Rose would not want everyone knowing how she had been manipulated by her last employer.

Next to him he could sense Sebastian was struggling to find the words, his normally loquacious friend for once unable to string together a sentence.

'We cannot help who we fall in love with,' Sebastian said eventually.

'I am not in love with her, but I do respect her.'

'I think you more than respect her.'

Richard thought of her kind eyes and her dazzling smile. He thought of her lips as they brushed against his and he thought of the way her body had felt underneath him that night she had come to comfort him as he slept.

'What does it matter?' he said dismissively. 'In a few months, at most a year, I will be gone.'

'You are the only one to make that decision. You don't have to leave. Stay, settle down, marry the damn maid if that's what you want. Allow yourself some happiness, some stability.'

For a moment he let himself imagine a future as his friend described it. He imagined waking up next to Rose every morning, of pulling her into his arms and leisurely making love. He imagined walking with his children through the meadows, teaching them to swim in the river and showing them how to fish. It was an idyllic dream, a tempting one, but not one he could allow.

He found himself wanting it, wanting all of it. It was a heady feeling and as he pictured the future, he thought he could feel happiness. Shaking his head, he pushed the image from his mind. It was tempting, but he had lost the chance of that life a long time ago.

'Think about it,' Sebastian said. 'Promise me that at least. Consider staying, consider letting go of the past and consider allowing yourself to be happy.'

Richard nodded, unable to find the words to explain how difficult it was to do even one of those things. For so long his whole life had been built around staying abroad, around the idea of penance, of suffering. It was impossible to even think another future was an option.

Chapter Nineteen

'There is something I need to do,' Mr Digby announced as he came through the door into his father's room.

Lord Digby was sitting in his chair, looking out over the garden. He had a book on his lap and every so often would pick it up and examine it, turning the pages, but never reading a word.

Rose looked up. In the twenty-four hours since they had shared a kiss on the bench overlooking the meadow, she had spent her time trying to avoid Mr Digby. If she heard him coming up the main stairs, she would quickly slip down the servants' stairs and when he had called in to see how his father fared she had made her excuses to take something down to the kitchen.

She felt embarrassed and every time she saw Mr Digby the embarrassment intensified a little more. The kiss was awkward enough, but it was her confession beforehand that really made her cringe. She had bared her heart to him, told him her deepest fears and let him know how much she cared for him, how much she wanted something more between them. The more she thought about what she had said the worse it seemed.

Now there was no escaping Mr Digby, standing as he was directly in front of her and holding her eye as he spoke.

'There is something I need to do and I would very much appreciate it if you would come with me.'

'Is it something for your father, Mr Digby?'

'No.' He glanced across at the old man. Mr Watkins was out of the room at the moment, so apart from Lord Digby they were alone. 'I am going to call on Mrs Godrum.'

Rose's eyes widened and immediately she forgot the awkwardness between them. For a moment she was too shocked to speak.

'I sent a note yesterday afternoon and received one back this morning saying she would receive me later this afternoon.' He cleared his throat and shifted a little before continuing. 'I was hoping you might come with me.'

'You want me to come with you to visit Mrs Godrum?'

'Yes.'

'Of course I will, if that is what you wish, but I do not understand why you need me. Is your father going, too?'

'No, it would be just you and me.' He glanced over his shoulder and then reached out for her hand. 'I have been trying to summon the courage to see Mrs Godrum ever since I returned home. It is a prospect that fills me with such dread you cannot imagine, yet I know I cannot put it off any longer.'

'I think it is a very brave thing to do.'

'I think having you there would make it all just a little easier,' he said softly, his normally decisive manner missing today and replaced with this uncertainty.

'I know I have no right to think of my own emotions, but I hoped you might accompany me. Your presence is calming, Rose. You make me feel more at ease and I think that will help with what I need to do today.'

'If you think I will help, then of course I will come.' She felt the stirring of anticipation deep inside him. A few days earlier she'd had to push him to talk to Lady Cambridgeshire. He had been too locked in his cycle of self-hatred and this need to punish himself that he couldn't see that even those most directly affected by the tragedy might have different thoughts on what had happened years on.

It would still be painful, but it wasn't so fresh and perhaps it would allow him to start to accept what had happened and work through his guilt. 'I will talk to Mr Watkins and, if you have no objections, ask one of the footmen to help with your father this afternoon, so he is never left alone.'

'Very good. I plan to leave just after two o'clock.'

Rose was distracted for the rest of the morning but two o'clock came round quickly and, once she had checked Mr Watkins had everything he needed for the afternoon, she made her way downstairs.

Outside, Mr Digby was standing holding the bridles of two horses, one a large gelding with a shiny black coat and another, much smaller mare.

'The grooms assure me Buttercup is the gentlest horse in the stable,' he said as he saw her expression of horror.

'I have never ridden a horse before.'

'I will help you up and then all you need to do is hold the reins and sit still in the saddle.'

She shook her head, taking a step back. 'We should take the carriage.'

'It is far too nice a day to take the carriage.'

'It is going to thunder later…the air is close, I can feel it.'

'Mrs Godrum only lives twenty-five minutes away. The clouds are hardly going to gather in the next hour and a half.'

Rose was fast running out of excuses and eyed the horse with distrust. She liked animals, but she didn't have much experience with them. When she was a child she had been petrified of the stray street dogs that would slink down the alleys searching for food. They were hungry and vicious and gave her an early fear of dogs.

When she had lived with the Wetherbys they had owned a beautiful brown spaniel with silky ears and a happy demeanour. He had done a good job in reversing the fear she'd felt around dogs, but apart from him she hadn't ever had much contact with animals and certainly nothing as big as a horse.

'This is not natural,' she muttered as she took a step closer to the horse, her stomach clenching with anxiety.

'There is nothing more natural than riding on horseback on a beautiful summer's afternoon.' He watched as she put out a tentative hand to stroke the horse on the nose. 'If you really do not want to ride, we can go by carriage, but I think once you get up there you will be fine.'

'If she bolts from underneath me, I will not be happy.'

'She will not bolt.'

'How do I get on?'

Even though she was the smallest, gentlest horse in the

stables, the grey mare was still a good size and Rose could not see how she could get all the way up to the saddle.

'Here,' Mr Digby said. 'You put your foot in my hand and I lift you up. Swing your other leg over as you go up.'

'Hardly dignified.'

'No one is watching.'

She felt him come up behind her, his body almost touching hers. As she looked over her left shoulder, her eyes caught his for a moment and a thrum of attraction passed between them. She thought of their last kiss, how she had promised herself it would be their last, cursing the desire that was building up from Mr Digby just standing a few inches away from her.

'Ready?'

'No,' she murmured.

'Up you go.'

It was inelegantly done, with Rose ending up with the skirt of her dress tucked between her legs, pinning her down. She was sprawled forward, clinging on to the horse's neck, and right now she didn't see how she would ever be able to let go. Even though the horse was classed as small she felt a long way from the ground and had visions of crashing down to the earth and breaking every bone in her body.

'Put your feet in the stirrups,' Mr Digby said. He was trying to suppress a smile, holding his face rigid so she did not see him laughing at her.

Carefully, she kicked out, too petrified to lean to one side or another to find out where the stirrups were.

'Here.' He gripped hold of one ankle and gently guided her foot into the stirrup. When he was sure that foot was in place he moved round to the other side.

'Now lift yourself up out of the saddle and then you can pull your skirt from underneath you.'

'How do you expect me to lift myself out of the saddle? I am not a magician.' She heard a note of hysteria in her voice and desperately tried to suppress it.

'Hold the reins to steady yourself and then just stand up in the stirrups.'

'You want me to stand up on the back of the horse?'

'I'm not suggesting you start performing acrobatics, Rose. I merely mean you could lift yourself up an inch or two to release the material of your skirt, so it is a little more comfortable. And a little less revealing.'

She glanced down and was horrified to see her dress was hitched up to well above her knees, exposing the soft skin of her calves and the lower half of her thighs. She pulled on the hem, but the material was well and truly caught on the saddle and by her sitting on it.

'Sit up straight and gently raise yourself out of the saddle.'

'You make it sound like an easy thing to do,' she grumbled.

'It is easy. Did you want me to hold you?'

She only hesitated a moment before nodding. Mr Digby put one hand on her hip and the other on her exposed thigh, holding her steady as she first sat up straight, then raised herself up. Rose felt every second of the contact as if his hand was setting her skin on fire, yet she felt bereft when he moved it to help her pull her skirts out from underneath her.

'Satisfied?' he asked once she was sitting back in the saddle.

She nodded, gripping the reins tightly.

'Relax your hands. Buttercup can feel the tension.'

'How can I relax my hands when I do not feel relaxed?'

She thought she saw Mr Digby suppress a smile as he turned away. He mounted easily, and within a minute they were ready to go.

'Go,' she muttered at her horse.

'Nudge her with the heels of your boots.'

'How does she know how fast I want her to go? What if she takes off at a gallop?'

'Nudge her gently.'

Rose tried a tiny nudge that did nothing and then tapped her heels against the horse's flank a little firmer. With docile, plodding steps, Buttercup set off at a sedate pace.

'Well done.'

'We don't have to go any faster, do we?'

'It depends if we wish to get there today or next week.' He smiled at her and shook his head. 'No, this pace is fine.'

'Good.'

'Do you know you are a marvellous distraction? I have been nervous about this visit all morning, yet the last ten minutes I have not thought of what is to come.'

'I am glad my discomfort served a purpose.'

'Perhaps you will be a master horsewoman soon—you could audition to join the circus at Astley's.'

'The most elegant acrobat on horseback there ever was.'

'We might have to work on your mounting first.'

They fell silent as they rode through the dappled shade of the drive and headed out into the lanes that led towards Hemingford Grey. There was a bridge there over the river and from there it was only a short ride to Houghton where Mrs Godrum lived.

'Lord Cambridgeshire saw us yesterday,' Mr Digby said as they rounded the bend and Hemingford Grey came into sight.

Rose stiffened, her body tense.

'He saw us on the bench?'

'Yes.'

She bit her lip. Lord Cambridgeshire was a kind man, a good man, but she was sure he would have an opinion on a liaison between Mr Digby and her.

'Do not fear, he will not say anything.'

'Are you certain?'

'I am.'

'I do not wish to lose my position.'

'I know what is at stake for you, Rose.'

'You told him there was nothing between us?'

'I have known the man since I was an infant, he would have seen the lie.'

She looked at him sharply.

'He thinks it is a passing fancy, that is all,' he said, glancing over at her.

'You told him it was just a moment of weakness?'

'I did.'

'You do not think he will tell anyone?'

'No. Cambridgeshire is discreet. Perhaps his wife, but she will hardly have an opinion on it.'

'You do not know what people can be like.' She bit her lip, worrying at it. Lady Digby was a fair woman and Rose thought she would overlook most minor indiscretions, but Mr Digby was the son she had not seen for years finally home. It was hardly a choice at all if she felt the atmosphere could become difficult.

They rode in silence again, crossing over the River Great Ouse and picking their way across another wild-flower meadow until the ancient watermill came into view.

'Mrs Godrum lives just at the edge of the village,' Mr Digby said, motioning to a row of sizeable houses built on a narrow road that led away from the village square.

'How are you feeling?'

'Truthfully? I want to turn back.'

'Just think—in an hour this will all be over. Whatever happens in the house, you will be back out here in the fresh air within the hour.'

They stopped, Rose pulling on the reins gently and waiting for Mr Digby to dismount and secure his horse before moving to her side. He reached up and lifted her off the horse, taking all of her weight before he set her gently on the ground. They stood body to body for a second before he quickly moved away.

The house was set back from the road and had a wooden gate painted white and a little fence surrounding the front garden. The front door was up a short set of steps and the whole house and garden was immaculately kept. Mr Digby was looking up at the front door with trepidation.

Rose walked over to stand next to him and slipped her hand into his. Right now she needed to put aside her own emotions. It was miraculous that he had decided to come and see Mrs Godrum, and perhaps even more remarkable that he had asked for her help. These last eight years he had shut everyone out, fled from the people who could give him love and support. He had manged to survive, but he most certainly had not thrived.

This morning he had reached out for the first time and asked for help. She didn't want to examine what it meant that he had asked *her* to accompany him—that would be spinning dreams out of empty air—instead, she decided to be thankful that he had managed to reach out. Perhaps there was hope for his future after all.

'My mistress is in the drawing room,' a maid said as she opened the door, waiting for them to come through the gate and up the steps. 'She's expecting you.'

There was no turning back now and Rose felt the tension pulsing from him in waves as he entered the house.

Richard felt sick and his vision had gone a little grey. The last time he had been here was to tell a family they had lost their only son, their pride and joy. It had been a horrific experience, one that he relived in his mind involuntarily, sometimes during his waking hours and sometimes when he was asleep.

Beside him, Rose squeezed his hand one last time as they went through the door, anchoring him to the present before she slipped from his grasp and allowed him to walk a couple of steps in front of her.

'Mr Digby is here, ma'am,' the maid said, watching them curiously as they passed.

Mrs Godrum must have been around the same age as his own mother, somewhere in her fifties and certainly not over sixty, yet she looked much older. The lines on her face were deep and her eyes hooded, making her look like a dozy owl. Her hair was fully grey and swept back into a severe bun. Even her shoulders were hunched and her fingers curled with rheumatism.

'Good afternoon,' Richard said, silently cursing as the words stuck in his mouth. His tongue felt heavy and all his movements slow.

'Come in, Mr Digby,' Mrs Godrum said, her voice stronger than he was expecting. Her eyes under their hoods were more lively than he had first thought, too, and he realised that her body might be frail, but her mind was lively. 'Who is this with you?'

'Miss Carpenter. She is a friend.'

'Come in, Miss Carpenter, have a seat. You, too, Mr Digby.'

Although he had known Frederick and Amelia Godrum since childhood, he realised he had only heard their mother speak on a handful of occasions. Her voice was low and sonorous, with a hint of a Norfolk accent.

'It has been a long time, Mr Digby.'

'Eight years.'

'Eight years, two months and four days,' Mrs Godrum said pointedly.

Richard inclined his head, feeling a wave of guilt threaten to overtake him. In the chair next to him, Rose leaned a little closer and, although she could not touch him here, under the watchful eye of Mrs Godrum, she placed her fingers on the arm of her chair so that they almost brushed against his.

'I heard your husband passed away. I am sorry for your loss.'

Mrs Godrum grunted, but didn't say anything, and Richard got the impression she had not mourned her husband much.

'I heard you have been out of the country this whole time,' Mrs Godrum said, her eyes travelling over him. 'So, you see the gossip works both ways. I hear of you and you hear of me.'

'I saw Lady Cambridgeshire a few days ago,' Richard said, trying a different approach.

Mrs Godrum's face softened. 'My darling Amelia. She's a good girl and all the grandchildren she has given me is a wonderful gift in my old age. Do you have children, Mr Digby?'

'No.'

'I thought not. It is a shame for your mother. I am sure she would want to be a grandmother.'

'She would.'

'I hope you are not holding off on my account.'

Richard blinked, unsure what to make of the woman's words. She was a little strange, her manner abrupt but not unfriendly. He put it down to her finding this meeting as difficult as he was, but it could also just be her way. Some people did withdraw into themselves after a tragedy and Frederick had been the favourite child of both his parents.

'I...'

'Amelia's husband tells me about you,' Mrs Godrum said, leaning forward in her chair. 'Lord Cambridgeshire. You were good friends, I think, and my Frederick.'

'Yes.'

'Lord Cambridgeshire tells me where you have been, what you are doing.' She fixed him with a hard stare. 'I never had you down as a coward, Mr Digby.'

Richard felt himself stiffen and realised Mrs Godrum was baiting him, but to what end he could not fathom.

'A coward?'

'Yes, running away all these years. Hopping from place to place so your guilt does not catch up with you.'

'My guilt has never left me.'

'Perhaps that is the problem, then. You have never been able to run fast enough.' Her words felt sinister, although she had a half-smile on her face, and Richard couldn't work out if his heightened emotions were making it impossible to listen to her words objectively or whether she was just acting strangely. 'Is that the plan? To keep running your whole life?'

He studied her and realised she wanted candour. She wanted him to confess the agony he was feeling. Perhaps she needed to hear that the death of her son had left a lasting impression on a life other than her own.

'I am running,' he said quietly. 'I am running all the time. I throw myself into the most physical of work so my mind and body are exhausted and at the end of the day they just shut down. Every night I relive that fateful day in my dreams and every morning I wake up wishing things were different. I have had no peace since Frederick died and I doubt I will until the end of my life.'

'Good,' Mrs Godrum said, sitting back in her chair, satisfied. For a long moment they stared at one another and then the older woman sighed. 'I harbour no malice towards you, Mr Digby, not any more. When Frederick first died I cursed your name every day and every night, I would fall to my knees and plead with God to take you instead of my son. Grief does terrible things to us, does it not?'

Richard nodded, wondering what she would say next.

He felt on edge, as if she might launch an attack from any direction at any time.

'I am sorry,' he said quietly. 'I am sorry I did not diffuse the argument in another way and I am sorry I went through with the duel.'

'Yes, I think you are,' Mrs Godrum said. 'I mean it when I say I harbour no malice towards you now. Over the years I have gathered every piece of information about how my son died. I have spoken to the doctor in attendance and to the young man who was Frederick's second. I have summoned them here on numerous occasions to hear their stories and do you know what I have concluded, Mr Digby?'

He shook his head.

'It was an accident. A terrible accident, but an accident all the same.'

Richard inclined his head. She was right, of course—the pistol misfiring and then releasing the bullet when Frederick had turned it to look down the barrel had been an accident. Yet it did not absolve him from the rashness of his actions, the prideful response to being challenged to a duel by a man who he had always considered a friend.

'Frederick challenged you to a duel—he could always be hot-headed and impulsive. You accepted. Then there was a terrible accident. My Frederick died, we lost a wonderful son and the Godrum heir...' She paused, her eyes fixed on his fully '...but there is no reason for your parents to lose their son as well.'

Her tone had softened, and he saw the maternal instinct in her coming to the fore. She struggled up out of her chair, wincing as her knees cracked as she straightened. Richard stood quickly as well, looking down at the old woman as she hobbled over to him. 'In fact, I think it would be disrespectful to my Frederick to continue as you have been. The tragedy shouldn't mean two young men's lives should be ruined completely.'

She stopped directly in front of him and reached out, taking his hand. Her skin was thin and the joints of her hand swollen, making the fingers bend round.

'I forgive you,' she said quietly. 'And I insist you forgive yourself.'

Richard was speechless as Mrs Godrum nodded at him, inclined her head to Rose and then walked from the room. He heard a little sob when she was halfway down the hall and realised she had left so he wouldn't see her cry.

'We should go,' Rose said, standing quickly and leading the way out of the room. Richard felt as though he had just been trampled by half a dozen horses, but managed to stagger after her.

Only once they were outside in the fresh air did he feel his pulse beginning to return to normal and the strange dizzy sensation leave him.

Chapter Twenty

They were walking over the meadow towards the small bridge that crossed the river between Houghton and Hemingford Abbotts, leading the horses. The afternoon was hot and sticky, and as the river gushed past, Rose had the urge to dip her toes in. The memory of falling in the water a few days earlier came to the front of her mind and she quickly pushed the idea of a paddle away.

Richard had been quiet. For the first ten minutes of the walk home she had let him stew in his own thoughts, but soon he would have to talk about what had just happened.

'Let us sit in the sunshine for a moment,' she said, motioning to a secluded spot close to the river.

Richard did not object, busying himself with tying the horses to a low tree branch, making sure they had enough length in their reins to bend and enjoy the grass.

Rose had chosen a spot where the river had split into multiple channels, with the main fast-flowing river in the middle, but then on each side was a shallow, trickling stream that eventually led back to the main body of water.

She sat down on the banks of one of the smaller streams and started to pull off her boots and stockings. Richard watched her, an amused smile on his lips, even though the smile did not reach his eyes. She hitched up her skirt and petticoats to her knees and dangled her feet off the low bank, inhaling sharply as they hit the icy water.

'Refreshing?'

'It is,' she said, forcing the muscles in her legs to relax so she could lower her feet in a little more. 'Join me.'

'It does look tempting.'

He sat down beside her and began to pull his boots off, sighing as he dipped his feet into the cool water.

'That was strange at Mrs Godrum's house, wasn't it?'

'Very strange,' he said, looking straight ahead at a spot on the other bank.

'I didn't imagine her like that.'

'It is not how I remembered her.' He shook his head. 'In truth, I hardly remembered her at all. Frederick's father was a force of nature, a cruel man, harsh and bombastic. His brash temperament meant Mrs Godrum faded into the background. On the rare occasion I saw her she was quiet, mousy.'

'She's not now.'

'No, she certainly said what she was thinking.'

'How do you feel?' Rose said, turning to face him. He was still looking away, so she studied his expression, seeing the turmoil on his face.

'Torn. I expected her to be angrier, to rail and rant at me.'

'She wasn't angry at all.'

'No, she wasn't, was she? She was sad and tired, but she wasn't angry. I think her fury must have faded over the years.'

'It was a long time ago.' Rose held up her hands as she saw his expression. 'I am not saying anyone should be over what has happened, I just mean emotions change over time.'

Not his emotions, though. He'd worked hard to keep everything the same, to feel the same guilt, the same sense of shame and sadness that he had immediately after accident.

'Perhaps you're right. A lot has happened since Frederick's death.'

'Her last words to you were interesting.'

Richard turned to Rose and raised an eyebrow. 'I wondered when you would bring them up.'

'She told you to forgive yourself. To move on and to make something of your life. Otherwise, it was a mockery of her son's memory.'

'She didn't use those exact words.'

'I'm summarising.'

Mr Digby let his head drop, and Rose desperately wanted to reach out to him. She could see he was in turmoil and she wanted nothing more than to take him in her arms and give him the comfort he so sorely needed. Yet she knew to protect them both it was better if she sat there sedately, barely able to touch him.

'Have I had this wrong, Rose? All this time I've been thinking about trying to do something worthwhile, something that gives back to the world because I helped to take something sacred from it. Yet by doing that, I have held back on living my life. I have been stuck in perpetual turmoil these past eight years, never allowing myself to move forward.'

'You went through something terribly traumatic,' she said softly, deciding to throw away all her resolutions not to touch him and reach out for his hand. 'I do not think berating yourself for how you reacted is helpful. None of us knows how we would react in such circumstances; it is something most people never go through.'

She took a deep breath, knowing the best thing for him was to hear the truth, no matter how hard it was.

'But I think you have done enough of that now. I think you have stoked the fire of your guilt for plenty of time. Now you need to look forward, not back, to honour Frederick by living your life.'

'Going back to my old way of living would just be self-indulgent.'

'I think if you go back, if you flee England again and live this nomadic lifestyle, never allowing yourself comfort, never building any lasting relationships, you will never be able to move on with your life.'

'Should I get to move on, though, Rose? Do I deserve it?'

'Only you can answer that, Mr Digby.'

'Richard,' he said. 'My name is Richard.'

'Richard.' She felt a thrill as his name passed over her tongue and tried hard to suppress it. It had been a highly emotional afternoon and she felt spent, and her role had been supportive only. Richard looked tired himself, but she was gladdened to see he was considering Mrs Godrum's words.

'Thank you for coming with me, Rose. I might still be standing outside working out what I wanted to say if you hadn't come along.'

'I am glad I could be of service.'

'More than of service,' he murmured, turning to her, his fingers squeezing hers. 'You are a good woman, Rose. Too good to be mixed up with my problems.'

She swallowed hard, realising what was likely to happen if she did not stop it. Emotionally, Richard was all over the place and right now could not be objective. The desire he felt for her was mixed up with all these other warring emotions and it made it harder to control.

His eyes searched hers, full of emotion, and then she saw something else flare in them. After a moment of hesitation, he leaned forward and brushed his lips against hers. Rose felt her heart soar and a deep desire thrum through her, and she realised how much she had wanted this to happen. Her body felt as though it was on fire and the sensation strengthened as Richard deepened the kiss.

He gripped hold of her, pulling her to him, and kissed her hard. His hands were in her hair, pulling at the pins and making the long locks fall down her back. The intensity of his kiss scared her a little and for a moment she wondered if she should pull away, then she lost herself in the moment and all rational thought was lost.

'You are bewitching, Rose,' he said as he pulled away for a moment, peppering kisses across her cheek and on to her neck. She let her head fall back in ecstasy as he found the sweet spot on her neck that sent jolts of pleasure to her core. 'I want to kiss every inch of you. I would wager you have the softest skin.'

Never had she surrendered herself entirely like this. Never had she allowed her desire to take over, to be her guiding force.

'Don't stop,' she murmured. If he stopped now, she knew all she would be left with was frustration and regret. Later she could deal with the consequences of this afternoon tryst, but right now she just wanted to enjoy it fully.

Gently, he toppled her backwards, laying her down in the long grass, kissing her all the time.

'I do not approve of your dresses,' he murmured as his fingers traced along the high neckline. 'They are made to keep someone out.'

'I think that is exactly the point of them.'

'Turn over.'

She flipped on to her stomach and felt his fingers on her back, unfastening the dress so he could open it up and reveal the layers underneath.

'Too many damn layers,' he muttered as she turned back over.

'Let me lift it off.' It was hard to do while half sitting, half lying, but eventually she managed to rid herself of the heavy dress and lay back on her elbows with only her chemise and petticoats. She loved the way he looked at her, loved the pure desire in his eyes, and with the anticipation building she waited for him to cover her body with his own.

He hesitated, leaned forward and then sat back on his haunches. 'I'm a cad,' he said eventually as he looked at her lying there. 'After everything you told me here, I am doing to you exactly what I promised never to do.'

Rose felt her hopes come crashing down.

'I'm sorry, Rose,' he said. 'I'm not being fair to you.'

She felt the prick of tears in her eyes and willed the droplets away, not wanting to let him see her cry.

'I want this,' she said in a whisper. 'I want you.'

'I cannot give you what you need, Rose,' Richard said with a groan. His eyes were flicking over her body, and she saw how difficult it was for him to hold himself back.

'What I need right now is you, for you to kiss me, to show me how much you want me.'

He let out a low, possessive growl and moved on top of her, kissing her hard. His hands slipped underneath her chemise and she felt his fingers dance across her smooth skin. His touch made her body arch up towards him, her movements instinctive, and soon he was teasing her, circling his fingers ever closer to her breasts.

Rose let out a soft moan and for an instant she wondered if they were safe here in the meadow. It was a quiet part of the world, but people did stroll along by the river and it was a beautiful day to be out.

All worries soon flew from her mind as Richard gripped the hem of her chemise and pulled it off over her head and then quickly pushed down her petticoats. She was naked in the sunshine and for a moment he sat back and admired her.

Rose felt her skin begin to flush under his gaze and she began to sit up, but gently he pushed her back down, shrugging off his jacket and cravat at the same time.

'You are perfect, Rose,' he said, unable to stop his eyes flicking over her body. He lowered her lips to her skin, starting at her collarbone and trailing his kisses lower until he took one nipple into his mouth. Rose cried out as jolts of pleasure shot through her body.

'What are you doing?' she said, her voice heavy with desire.

'Do you not like it?'

'Don't stop.'

She saw him smile and then dip his head again, his teeth grazing her other nipple, making her gasp.

She should have felt exposed and vulnerable, lying naked as she was in the middle of the meadow, but Rose relished the cool breeze on her skin and she hardly felt naked with Richard's body covering hers. As he kissed and teased her, she ran her hands underneath his shirt, lifting it off over his head.

'I want you, Rose,' he murmured in her ear, and she knew this was the moment that would change everything between them.

'I want you, too.'

Quickly, she fumbled with the waistband of his breeches, pushing them down, and suddenly she felt his hardness against her. He paused to kiss her again and then pressed forward. Rose gasped as he went deeper and deeper, until her hips came up to meet his.

Together they found a rhythm, their bodies moving as if in a more and more frantic dance. Rose felt a wonderful heat building up inside her and every time Richard pressed into her, she thought it might make that heat explode. Just as she could tell he was getting close, she felt the burst of pleasure and then waves of pure bliss passed through her body. Above her Richard stiffened and then collapsed on top of her.

After a moment he rolled to one side, making sure not to crush her underneath him. Rose allowed herself to languish in the wonderful warm glow she was feeling, closing her eyes and not allowing any other thoughts in.

'We should dress, Rose,' Richard said, kissing her gently on the bare skin of her shoulder. 'We do not want to risk lying here with no clothes any longer—we have already been lucky no one has passed by.'

She didn't want this moment to end even though she knew he was right. The last thing they needed was a local to be out for a stroll and find them naked in the long grass. The gossip would be around the villages by nightfall.

Quickly, they dressed. Richard was silent and the pensive look had returned to his face. Rose wanted to reach out to him, to seek some sort of reassurance, but she wasn't sure what for. She had told him she wanted nothing more than their moment of pleasure and, in that moment, it had been the truth, but now they were heading back to Meadow View she couldn't help but wonder what the future held.

Once they were dressed and presentable, he helped her to mount Buttercup, his hands lingering on her waist and his lips coming down to kiss the bare skin of her neck.

They rode in silence, the tension between them mounting with every yard they got closer to Meadow View. Rose was uncertain if Richard had been so overwhelmed by the warring emotions after the visit to Mrs Godrum that he had sought a way to relieve the tension he was feeling, or if their intimacy was part of his new resolve to move on with his life.

She told herself it did not matter, that soon enough she would know, but she felt uneasy in her ignorance.

Before they entered the drive, she pulled on Buttercup's reins and brought the horse to a stop.

'What now?' she said, turning to Richard.

He must have known the question was coming for he took a long, measured breath.

'I do not know, Rose. I have a lot of thinking to do about my future.'

She felt her hopes shrivel inside her and realised quite how much she had wanted him to slip from his horse, fall to his knees and ask her to be his wife. It was a ridiculous notion, one that could never come true, but she realised now it was what she had been hoping for all along.

'Let me know when you decide,' she said, then pressed her heels into Buttercup's flanks more firmly than she meant to. The little horse sprang forward and started up the drive in a canter. Rose just about managed to hold on, her body tipping back on a couple of occasions, but thankfully she managed to right herself.

She brought the animal under control, arriving at the stables with Buttercup travelling at a more sedate pace. The grooms were at her side immediately and this time she didn't wait for Richard's help to dismount, accepting the assistance one of the grooms offered her to slip off the horse's back. Before Richard had even entered the stable yard, she had hurried inside, her cheeks burning from the humiliation she was feeling.

Chapter Twenty-One

As the carriage rolled to a stop outside the house, Richard was surprised to see Rose come out the front door. The past two days, she had spent her time avoiding him. She was good at it, slipping past him if he came into a room, ensuring she was never left alone with him, even ignoring a direct summons to his study.

Richard was careful not to corner her, remembering what she had said about her old employer and not wanting to conjure the bad memories, yet he had been desperate to talk to her. For two days he had seen her unhappy, drawn face and he knew he was the one solely responsible for her unhappiness.

What had happened between them had been completely unplanned. As they sat by the gurgling stream, he had felt a surge of hope. Hope that perhaps with time he could learn to forgive himself for his role in Frederick's death. Hope that he would learn to overcome the need to punish himself, to do penance. Hope that perhaps one day he might be able to settle down and lead some semblance of a normal life.

If he was honest, these thoughts had been bubbling inside him for a few days before the visit to Mrs Godrum's house. Ever since he had first discussed his guilt with Rose, he had felt some of the weight lift from his shoulders and again after she had encouraged him to talk to Amelia. The visit to Mrs Godrum had solidified those thoughts and made him realise that if Frederick's mother could forgive him, perhaps it was possible to forgive himself and move forward with his life.

As they had left the older woman's house, he had felt this great weight lift from his shoulders and for the first time in a long time it had felt as though anything was possible. When they had sat down by the gurgling stream, he had looked over at Rose and all the desire and the attraction had come bursting to the surface, and it had felt that for the first time he was in a position to do something about it. He had acted without fully thinking through the consequences, without knowing what the longer-term plan was, and now he had ruined things with Rose.

She stood stiffly beside him, waiting for Lady Digby to step down from the carriage. Her face was expressionless, her eyes fixed on a point in the distance and never wavering towards him.

'Richard, darling, you do not know how happy it makes me to come home and see you here waiting for me,' Lady Digby said, beaming at him. She looked well-rested, her eyes sparkling and her cheeks a little plumper. It seemed as though his aunt had cared for her well. 'And, Rose, it is a delight to see you as always. How is Lord Digby?'

'He is settled today, my lady. He slept well last night and is happy this morning in his glasshouse.'

'I am glad to hear it. It is a wonderful relief to know I can go away for a few days and my beloved Henry is fine without me.'

'He certainly missed you,' Rose said softly, 'but we were able to distract him.'

'She is an angel, isn't she?' his mother said, turning to Richard.

'An angel,' he repeated, his voice low.

Rose's eyes flicked to him, but she showed no emotion on her face. He wanted to reach out for her, to take her hand, but he could see such an advance would be completely unwelcome here. He would have to continue to try to catch her on her own so they could talk in private.

'I think I will go and see Henry straight away—will you both accompany me?' Lady Digby said, beaming at them. She seemed oblivious to the tension between them, but Richard knew they would have to be careful. His mother was an astute woman and she would pick up on any unusual behaviour quickly.

He offered his mother his arm, and together they walked around the side of the house to the gardens. Rose followed a few paces behind, presenting the perfect picture of a demure servant.

Mr Watkins rose from his seat beside Lord Digby and bowed as they entered the greenhouse. The normally well-presented man was a little hot and bothered, with beads of sweat forming on his forehead and his hair pushed up into tufts. It was unreasonably warm in the glasshouse, but Lord Digby either did not notice or did not mind.

'Henry, darling, I am home,' Lady Digby said and was rewarded with a distracted smile from her husband.

'Where have you been?' Lord Digby said.

'Running errands, nothing more.'

She took a seat beside her husband, and Richard watched with affection as his father explained at length what he was doing with the seedlings. The conversation was circular and repetitive, but not once did his mother lose patience with his father.

He took a step back and then another, thinking he would leave them to spend a little time together, but as he stepped back, he barrelled into Rose. She stumbled to one side, putting her hand out to save her from tripping, and winced as her palm caught on the sharp metal edge of the door. She let out an injured cry, but raised a hand to her mouth to muffle the sound as much as possible.

'Are you hurt?' he said, taking her hand immediately. There was a deep gash across the palm, only an inch long, but the blood was welling up from it at an impressive rate. 'We need to bind it.'

Quickly, he took off his cravat and wound it round her hand, not listening to any of her protestations. Only once the hand was bound and the bleeding had stopped did he pause for a moment.

As he glanced up, he caught the curious expression on his mother's face. He wondered if he had acted inappropriately towards Rose, but thought his actions were of one concerned person to another, nothing more.

'I will take Miss Carpenter back to the house,' he said, trying to sound as formal and officious as possible.

'No need to trouble yourself, Father.' Lord Digby had begun to stand up, but settled down at Richard's reassurance. He placed a hand under Rose's elbow to guide her out, but she quickly shrugged him off.

'I'm fine,' she said sharply. 'There is no need to fuss.'

She stalked out in front of him, and Richard saw his mother glance up with a slight frown on her face. He followed Rose out, only catching up when she was almost back at the house.

'Slow down,' he said, reaching out for her.

'Do not touch me.' She spun to face him, her eyes bright with defiance. 'You have no right to touch me.'

He let his hand drop to his side, but did not move away, instead leading her into the kitchens. Silently, he organised some water to be heated so he could clean the wound and for some bandages to be fetched.

'I am sure Mrs Green is perfectly capable of seeing to my wound,' Rose said as he took her hand in his own and began to unwrap the bandage.

'I have seen my share of injuries these last few years. Mrs Green is busy; I will clean and dress it.'

'Fine. Be quick. I have a lot to do this morning.'

She sat back in her chair, refusing to meet his eye, her expression only changing as he dabbed at the deep cut with a damp cloth, making sure there were no little pieces of dirt that could make the wound fester.

'It is still bleeding a little,' he said, pressing some dry cloth against it. 'I just need to hold this on here for a few minutes.'

She didn't reply.

'Rose,' he said, softly but firmly, 'we need to talk about what happened.'

'No.'

'We do.'

'Here is hardly the right place.'

They were sitting in the kitchen in a little alcove to one side. At that moment the rest of the kitchen was empty with Mrs Green outside choosing the best eggs from the chickens, but a maid or footman could enter at any time.

'There is no one else here and we will hear if anyone is approaching. I would say it is as good a place as any.' In an ideal world he would take her into his study and close the door, ensuring true privacy, but he'd been trying to do that these last couple of days and she had evaded him at every turn.

'What is there to say? It was a monumental mistake; one we shall not be repeating. I will let you know if there are any consequences.'

His eyes widened a little and he realised he had not even considered the fact that she might get pregnant.

She let out a low, humourless laugh. 'Do not fear, I think the chances are low. You will not have to be shackled to me by a child.'

'I am sorry about how it happened,' he said, hoping to catch her eye, but she was resolutely not looking at him.

'I doubt it. You got what you wanted.'

'That is not true, Rose. Not true and not fair.'

'Fine.' She looked up at him then and he saw the anguish in her eyes. 'I told myself it was fine to give in to my desires because it was my decision,' she said quietly. 'Mine alone. I knew the consequences, I knew what I would be giving up and I still chose to do it. No one forced me. There was no coercion.'

He could see she was thinking back to the awful time she had spent in a relationship with Mr Rampton, under his control in so many ways.

'I stand by that. We were two people who were overcome by the emotions of the afternoon and sought a way to get rid of some of the tension. Never did I expect or ask for anything more than that.'

'No,' he said, leaning in a little closer, 'you didn't.'

'But would it have been too much to ask for you to talk to me afterwards?'

'It was badly done, Rose, I am sorry. I was overwhelmed by everything that had happened that afternoon and I think I got caught up in my own head. You're right, I should have talked to you.'

'I knew what you would say, but it would have been nice to have had the clarity, to not be left wondering what on earth had happened and whether it changed anything.'

'Do you want it to change anything?' he asked, and her eyes snapped to his. He saw the turmoil there, the unspoken emotions fighting to get out. For a moment, he thought she was going to tell him she wanted a life with him, wanted to marry and settle down and raise a family together. Her lips parted and she almost started to speak, but then after a few seconds she closed her mouth and shook her head. 'Things are fine as they are.'

Richard let his head drop forward as he checked on the bleeding underneath the cloth he was holding to her hand. Gently, he removed it and started to wind the bandage around tightly so it would hold the dressing in place.

'You have always spoken the truth to me, Rose,' he

said as he worked. 'Even when it has been difficult for me to hear. Tell me the truth now.'

'You want me to declare my feelings when you know you feel nothing substantial in return. You want me to bare my soul, to tell you that I love you, just to be pushed away, rejected.'

Sharply, she pulled her hand away and part of the bandage began unravelling. Richard gently took it back, using the time he needed to fasten the end of the bandage, to gather his thoughts.

'You love me?'

'How can I love you? I barely know you. And I am a sensible woman. I would never fall in love with a man who is clearly living in the past.'

There were tears in her eyes now, and he wanted to reach out and pull her into his arms, but he knew he could not do so until he was completely sure of what he wanted. Right now, he desired Rose, not just through physical attraction, but he wanted to nurture the connection they had, the way she challenged him and made him feel alive for the first time in years.

Yet he was all too aware of what she had been through before. It would be beyond cruel to lead her on, make false promises and then in a few weeks or months find that he could not commit to a future with her.

She had told him what she wanted for herself—a nice man who would treat her as his equal, someone she could share her life with. It would be difficult for him to offer her that, but not impossible, yet he could not offer her anything if one day soon he pulled it away, deciding he was not ready to move forward with his life.

'I understand how difficult this is, Rose, and I am sorry I cannot give you the assurances you need.'

She scoffed and stood up, wincing as she caught her hand on the edge of the table.

'Sit down for a moment, please, Rose. We cannot leave things like this.'

'What more is there to say?' She didn't sit, but she didn't leave either, so he stood and faced her.

'I am reeling from being back here in England, from realising that perhaps my way of dealing with things these last eight years has not been the healthiest. I am having to reconsider how I live my life and what my plans for the future hold. I do not know if I am going to stay in England once my father has passed away, I do not know if I ever will be able to move forward enough to have even a semblance of a normal life. I cannot ask you to commit to a man who is this uncertain about his future.'

'Will you consider one question?'

He nodded, although he sensed it would be an uncomfortable one.

'When we were intimate,' she said slowly, her eyes flicking away from his for a second before coming back, 'what did you think would happen between us after?'

He shifted uncomfortably. She was right to ask it, although the answer was not one he was proud of.

'I wasn't thinking, Rose, not past the immediate satisfaction we could give one another. I wanted you and that was all that filled my mind. These last few weeks I have struggled to keep my distance. I have wanted to kiss you every time we talked, to hold you in my arms and feel the softness of your body. Yesterday I gave in to the desire I felt for you and I blocked out any thought of the possible consequences.'

Rose nodded, and he could see it was not the answer she had hoped for.

'I am not proud of what I did. I know I took advantage of you.'

'No,' she said sharply. 'I made my own decision. I wanted you, too.'

She turned and walked briskly away, ignoring him as he called after her.

Chapter Twenty-Two

Rose wiped the tears from her eyes and regarded herself in the little mirror above the writing desk on her wall. Her eyes were puffy and red-rimmed and her cheeks sallow. It would be obvious to anyone who saw her that she had been crying, but she hoped she would be able to fool people into thinking it was because of the cut on her hand.

'Damn you, Richard Digby,' she muttered under her breath. After she had left Mr Rampton's house over two years ago she had told herself she would never let a man make her cry again. Richard was different to her last employer: he did not seek to control her or coerce her, yet he had hurt her all the same.

Rose shook her head, aware it was partly her fault as well. She had seen the change in him after he had come out of Mrs Godrum's house. It was as if a weight had been lifted from his shoulders. Of course, there was a lot to think about, but she could see that forgiveness from Frederick Godrum's mother had been important to him, perhaps important enough to finally allow him to move on from the tragedy that had overshadowed his life for the last eight years.

She hadn't expected him to change everything immediately, but she had been caught up in the hope that he would be open to a loving relationship and she might be the one to give that to him. He had wanted human contact, for he had starved himself of it for years, to give in to the desire that flowed through both of them. She didn't regret making love to him, but she did regret her expectations of what might happen after.

It had been devastating when he had gone silent, hardly looking at her. Quickly, she had realised there would be no declaration of love, no proposal or promise that they would have a future together. Rose had only realised quite how much she had wanted this when it hadn't materialised, so the last few days she had worked hard to avoid him.

Their conversation today had drained her of any hope she had still harboured. Richard was not ready for a relationship and, even if he was, he was not sure he would choose her. He had told her the first part and she had been able to surmise the second part from what he hadn't said.

It was a devastating blow and up here in her room she had sobbed for the future she had secretly pined for. Now she needed to close off that emotional part. She still had a home and a wonderful employer. She had a job she enjoyed and slowly she was building up a little in savings. She would have to work out how to continue with her job with Richard around, but she was strong and capable, and she would manage somehow.

With some effort she put on a smile as she walked

into Lord and Lady Digby's room. Lord Digby was covered in soil from the glasshouse, but he seemed to be happy, no doubt because Lady Digby was back home.

'Shall I fetch some water to get you cleaned up?' Rose said as she breezed into the room.

'That would be wonderful,' Lady Digby said as she turned to face Rose, her expression changing as she caught sight of her. 'Rose, dear, whatever is the matter?'

'My hand hurts a little,' Rose said, trying to act nonchalant. She prided herself on telling the truth. People got hurt by lies and deception and she had decided a long time ago not to be a part of it, yet sometimes life required you to tell little white lies, just like the ones she told to Lord Digby to calm his agitation. She had always thought she was good at these, skilled in the art of balancing the need to only give a little information away without piquing someone's interest.

Today it would seem her skills had abandoned her as Lady Digby looked dubiously at the bandaged hand.

'Mr Watkins, help Lord Digby get changed,' Lady Digby said, moving over to Rose and taking her by the arm. 'We are going to have a little talk.'

It took all of Rose's self-control not to burst into tears as Lady Digby led her down to the small morning room at the south-east corner of the house. It had beautiful big windows that looked out over the countryside and bathed the room in morning light. It was not a large room, with space for two armchairs and a comfortable sofa. Lady Digby closed the door behind them and sat on the sofa, patting the empty cushion beside her.

Rose sat, pressing her lips together to try to stop the

tears that were threatening to fall. If Lady Digby said anything nice or supportive, she would burst into tears.

'This isn't like you, Rose,' she said, and Rose felt the older woman's penetrating gaze on her. 'Even when you trapped your hand in that awful heavy trunk you barely made any fuss. Are you sure there is nothing else going on?'

She didn't want to lie to Lady Digby, but she had no other choice. Her employer might be kind and understanding, but that did not mean she would condone even a failed liaison between one of her servants and her son.

'I haven't seen you like this since you first arrived at Meadow View, after you had run away from that vile man.'

'I am fine, Lady Digby, thank you for your concern. I will be able to get back to work straightaway.'

'Is it a young man? Has someone broken your heart, Rose?'

'No,' she said, sniffing. 'I would not be foolish enough to risk my heart, my lady, not after I got so entangled before.'

Lady Digby smiled at her sadly. 'You should not swear off love, my dear. It can bring a wonderful contentment to your life.' Suddenly, the older woman's eyes narrowed. 'It is Richard, isn't it?'

Rose felt panic rising up inside, threatening to take over. If Lady Digby guessed what had happened between them, Rose might be looking for a new position as soon as tomorrow.

'No,' she said quickly.

'He speaks without thinking sometimes. What has he done? I warned him not to upset you.'

It was heartwarming to hear Lady Digby be so protective of her, but Rose did not think it would continue if she knew the truth.

'We clashed a few times when you were away, but each time we worked it out. He has been very helpful, my lady.'

'Yet there was a tension between you in the glasshouse, a distance.'

'We have different ways of doing things.'

For over a minute, Lady Digby sat and regarded Rose, the silence stretching out between them. Rose felt as though the older woman was reaching into her mind and pulling out all of her darkest secrets and it took all of her self-resolve not to squirm.

'Do you know, when Richard was young, I was convinced he would marry Amelia Godrum. They were good friends and she was a few years younger and from a good local family. It seemed like a perfect match.'

'This is Lady Cambridgeshire now?'

'Yes. Amelia is a lovely girl, demure and sweet and dutiful. She makes Lord Cambridgeshire very happy, but she would not have been the right choice for my Richard.'

Rose felt her mouth and lips going dry and her breathing become shallower. Lady Digby couldn't know anything for sure, but why was she talking about Richard's choices of wife?

'On paper she sounds like the perfect match: she is accomplished in womanly pursuits and is from a family that can trace their heritage back generations. She and Richard were even amiable. Yet a marriage between them would not have worked.' Lady Digby sighed. 'You are probably wondering what point I am trying to make.'

Rose inclined her head, not trusting her voice enough to say anything out loud.

'Sometimes a person is more than what they appear on paper. A gentleman who spends his time raising funds for an orphanage, a lady who runs a successful business. These are snippets of who people are, but it is not the whole sum. Sometimes if you look at a list of two people's attributes you think they are from different worlds with nothing in common. It is only when you see them together that you realise how well their characters complement each other.'

'I am not sure I follow you, Lady Digby.'

'No, I am not sure I am making sense.' Lady Digby turned to her and laid a hand on Rose's knee. 'Perhaps I should be more straightforward.' She took a deep breath, 'I admire you, Rose. I know how hard you have worked to get where you are now, what you have overcome. I admire your perseverance and your strength of character. To me, those attributes are much more important than the circumstances of your birth.'

'Thank you,' Rose said, the tears welling up in her eyes again.

'*Any* mother should be proud to welcome you into the family.'

Rose closed her eyes and let the tears fall on to her cheeks. Lady Digby's kindness and generosity overwhelmed her. She had skirted round the subject, conscious of Rose's desire not to discuss it, but at the same time given Rose enough reassurance that she knew, whatever happened, Lady Digby would ensure she was welcomed and cared for.

'Right, enough of that. Let us go and get Lord Digby cleaned up, otherwise he'll be eating his meal with soil all over his hands.'

Richard walked quietly into the room to find his father snoring gently on the bed and his mother sitting in a chair at the bedside, reading a book.

'Come sit with me,' she said, motioning for him to bring another chair over. 'I missed you while I was away.'

'And I you.'

'It is so good to have you back, Richard. I know you cannot change anything, but I feel so much better with you just being here.' She squeezed his knee. 'It must be quite an adjustment.'

'It is in some ways, but in others it feels as though I have never been away.'

'I do not want to press you, but have you decided to stay for a little while at least?'

Richard hesitated and saw the suppressed hope in his mother's face. 'I am not planning on leaving any time soon,' he said with a gentle smile.

'Good.'

'I went to see Mrs Godrum a few days ago.'

He could see this had thrown his mother. She opened and closed her mouth a few times, but no words came out.

'How is she keeping?' she asked eventually.

'I think her joints pain her, she has rheumatism by the looks of it and she is struggling a little to get around. She seemed a little melancholy, but no more than to be expected.'

'What did she say to you?'

'That I was wasting my life.'

His mother's eyes widened. 'She used to be blunt when we were younger. I've known her since we were children, although she was a few years older than me. She was a little odd back then, but then she married that horrible brute of a man and for years she was nothing more than his shadow, sometimes glimpsed but never heard.'

'She has her voice now.'

'Was she sharp with you?'

'In a way, but I do not think she meant to be un-kind—quite the opposite, really.'

Lady Digby studied him carefully. 'What do you think?'

'I am not sure,' he said with a sigh. 'All these years I thought I was travelling the world to try to do some good, to balance out the poor decisions and the subse-quent tragedy, but what if it was purely selfish? What if I was running away, immersing myself in other peo-ple's problems so I did not have to think about my own?'

'Oh, my darling boy, you have to stop punishing yourself. You experienced something extremely trau-matic at a young age. Then Mr Godrum drove you from the country and it meant you were on your own, without anyone who loved you to help, trying to deal with ev-erything that had happened. Is it any surprise that you reacted in a slightly strange way, thinking of penance and how best to repent?'

'I suppose not. Yet it had been eight years, Mother—eight years of thinking this was the best way to cope with things.'

'You are alive and healthy, Richard. Yes, your life has been very different to what you had planned these last eight years, but you have a chance now to think about what you want from your future, what you really want.'

'And if I decide to go back to the poorer parts of the world?'

'If that is your decision, and you make it with your eyes open, knowing what you do now, then that is what you are meant to do.' She squeezed his knee affectionately. 'Equally if you decide to settle here in England, to marry and have children, that is where your journey had taken you, too. *Whoever* the young lady happens to be.'

It was a strange turn of phrase and he looked at his mother sharply, wondering if she could suspect there was something between him and Rose. She hadn't been there, so it was difficult to see how she could work out their relationship was more than one of brief acquaintances, yet his mother was scarily intuitive when it came to matters of the heart.

Richard closed his eyes. He had a lot of thinking to do. Only once he had worked out what his future held, whether he could learn to live with his guilt and build a semblance of a normal life or whether he needed to move on again, could he talk to Rose about their future. He only hoped he wasn't too late.

Chapter Twenty-Three

As Richard walked through the village, he looked up at the sky. Today was another remarkably hot day. The air was close and the clouds heavy and it felt as though finally at any moment the weather was going to break. Soon there would be rain and perhaps even a storm to get rid of the humidity that made him feel as though he were back in the tropics.

He pushed open the gate to the church, following the path for a short way and then making his way across the grass, skirting respectfully around the edges of the graves. The one he was looking for was in the corner of the graveyard, near the perimeter wall. A few feet away, a beautiful pink rose bloomed, and in the heat many of the petals had fallen off and lay scattered across the grave.

Crouching down, he read the inscription on the gravestone.

Frederick Edmund Godrum
1789-1809
Beloved son and brother

*Taken too soon from these earthly plains
and welcomed into heaven*

The grave was beautifully maintained with no hint of lichen on the stone and no weeds in the grass. In contrast, next to Frederick's grave was his father's. It was only a couple of years old, but already it looked neglected. The headstone was made of a poorer quality stone than Frederick's and it was cracked across the top, and the grass was long and overgrown and filled with weeds. Richard wondered if this was Mrs Godrum's little revenge on a husband who had controlled and belittled her for so long.

'Good afternoon, Frederick,' he said, wondering whether his old friend was listening from somewhere up in heaven. 'Eight years, it is a long time, is it not?' On his way over, he had thought of what he would have wanted to say to his friend if he had the chance, but now all the words had abandoned him and instead he felt the visceral roil of emotion.

Reaching out, he touched the gravestone to anchor himself and sternly told himself to get a grip on reality.

'I came to say sorry, Frederick. Every day of the last eight years I have wished I did something different and I expect I will wish that for the rest of my life. I used to think the guilt was impossible to live with, but I'm coming to realise it is just part of me, part of the man I am.' He shook his head, allowing the memories to flood over him. Of playing as young boys, splashing in the shallows of the river, of growing up together and getting drunk, of arguing good naturedly over cards. 'I wish things had been different,' Richard said, and then stood.

He took one last look at the gravestone and walked away across the graveyard.

'I wish things could be different,' he murmured under his breath. It was the truth and something he wished for every single day.

As he walked away from the grave, he felt a weight lifting from his shoulders and he knew in that moment what he needed to do with his life. It was as if the mist had cleared from in front of his eyes and he could finally see what was right in front of him.

There was a slight spring in his step as he walked through the gates of Meadow View, but his sense of peace was shattered when from behind him there was a clattering of hooves. Doctor Griffiths appeared on horseback, riding fast, and Richard had to jump out of the way to avoid being trampled. The doctor shouted an apology as he passed, but most was whipped away by the wind.

Following behind Dr Griffiths, riding almost as fast, was one of the grooms, a young man by the name of Peterson. He reined in his horse when he saw Richard.

'What is Dr Griffiths doing here?'

'Lord Digby had a fall, sir. He hit his head. Lady Digby sent me for the doctor.'

The drive was not overly long and Richard set off at a run immediately, bursting through the front door a minute later. Two maids were gathered in the hall, looking worried, and they both curtsied when they saw him.

'Is Dr Griffiths upstairs?'

'Yes, sir,' one of the maids said. 'Lady Digby is there, too, and Rose.'

He took the stairs two at a time, making the short journey from front door to bedroom in no time at all. Making himself pause before he opened the door, aware the scene could be devastating inside, he breathed deeply before knocking and entering.

His father was in the bed, eyes closed. His chest rose and fell steadily, but as Richard watched there was no change in the expression on his face and no movement in his limbs.

Lady Digby sat holding her husband's hand while the doctor examined him.

Rose was standing to one side. As he entered the room, she saw him and hurried over, her expression one of concern. She had been avoiding him again, slipping from the room any time he entered. She had remained stony faced and unemotional, but he knew how much she was hurting. Soon he would have to tell her how he felt, tell her what he wanted for the future, but now was not the right time.

'What happened?' he murmured as she approached. She touched him lightly on the elbow, guiding him over to the bay window that looked out over the gardens and the river beyond.

'Your father was pacing around, as he does. I was downstairs, bringing up his tray of mid-morning tea, but Mr Watkins and your mother were here in the room with him. He tripped on the edge of the rug and was unable to regain his balance...' She paused, glancing over to the bed. 'He knocked his head on the edge of the table and has not regained consciousness since.'

Richard watched his father's frail, lined face for a

moment, wondering if the old man could survive such an insult.

'What does Dr Griffiths say?'

'He is still examining Lord Digby…he hasn't said anything yet.'

Rose swallowed and he could see there was more.

'What is it, Rose?'

'He must have hit his head hard. There was an awful lot of blood.'

In his life he had known of several people who had hit their heads and been knocked unconscious. There seemed little rhyme or reason as to who woke up relatively unscathed and who did not.

'Go and be with him,' Rose said, her expression softer than he had seen in days.

He walked across the room, his heart thumping in his chest. He didn't want to see pain in his father's expression, but as he got closer he saw Lord Digby looked peaceful, almost as if he was just sleeping.

'Ah, Mr Digby, I am glad you are here,' Dr Griffiths said. 'The maid has explained what happened?'

'Yes, Miss Carpenter has told me. What do you think, Doctor?'

'The impact has rendered him unconscious. There is a nasty wound on his scalp, but thankfully it is not too deep. I can dress that; the main issue is whether the knock on his head has caused any bleeding inside his brain.'

'How can you tell?'

'I can't. It is a matter of time only. Now we must watch and wait. If there is bleeding, then he will not wake up. Slowly, the pressure from the blood on the brain will make his whole body shut down.' Doctor Griffiths must have seen the expression of horror on their faces, for he continued quickly. 'Please do not worry too much. Lord Digby cannot feel any of this. Here…watch.'

He took out a metal pin, about two inches in length, and pointed at one end. With a measured gesture he pricked Lord Digby on the back of his hand.

'See? He does not even flinch.'

'And if there is no bleeding?'

'Then hopefully he will wake up, but there is nothing I can do to speed up the process.'

'Thank you, Doctor,' Lady Digby said.

Rose stepped forward. 'What should we do about feeding him and keeping him hydrated?'

'Nothing. If you try to feed him, he will choke.'

'Will he not waste away?'

Doctor Griffiths shrugged. 'Sometimes we have to choose the least risky of two paths. We cannot be sure he will waste away, but I am certain he will choke if you try to feed him while he is unconscious.' The doctor paused and looked from Richard to his mother and back again. 'Lord Digby is gravely ill, but I know he will be well cared for in this house.'

'Thank you, Doctor,' Richard said. 'We shall send a messenger if anything changes.'

'Good. I will return tomorrow, but you can reach me at home if you need me in the meantime.'

Lady Digby went to rise, but Richard motioned for her to stay put. 'I will walk Dr Griffiths out; you stay with Father.'

'Thank you.'

Richard waited while the doctor gathered his equipment into his bag and then led the way out of the room. Downstairs, Dr Griffiths paused by the door.

'It is a very bad bump to the head, Mr Digby. I did not wish to worry your mother unnecessarily, but I would urge you to make sure all your father's affairs are in order.'

'Thank you, Doctor.'

The next three days were a blur of worry and watchful inactivity. Lady Digby temporarily moved from the shared bedroom into one of the guest bedrooms and they then took it in turns to sit with Lord Digby, ensuring that between him, his mother and Rose there was always someone in the chair beside his bed, ready to be a comforting presence should he wake.

For three days there was no change, except every time Richard entered the room it seemed as though his father was getting a little frailer. His body had little fat on it anyway, but now his face was looking gaunt and his skin sallow.

'Go get some rest,' Rose said as she came into the room.

The tension between them had been suspended while they navigated this latest tragedy and Richard was glad of it. Soon, he needed to talk to Rose, but now was not the right time. She had lost some of her iciness towards him, returning to a formal way of interacting, calling him Mr Digby, but she was supportive all the same.

'I will change his sheets and then sit with him for a while.'

'Thank you. I do feel weary.'

He stood and stretched. He had been reading through

some of the estate accounts, making little notes in the margins of questions he wanted to ask the steward who handled all the properties and rents. It was bright in the room, but still his eyes felt strained and tired.

'You look tired, Mr Digby,' Rose said, a note of concern in her voice.

'I have not been sleeping well,' he said, gathering up the papers. 'And you used to call me Richard.'

'I do not think that is appropriate any more.'

He wanted to reach out for her, to banish the cold civility in her tone, to enfold her in his arms and take comfort from her as well as give it.

'Perhaps not,' he said. 'At least until things are sorted between us.'

She turned away, but even before she did there wasn't even a flicker of interest.

'I need to change the sheets now,' she said, her tone flat. 'I hope you manage to rest without any nightmares.'

'Thank you.'

He hesitated for a moment, hating how he had let things deteriorate between them. He wanted to sweep her into his arms, to kiss her and show her how much she meant to him, but now was not the right place or the right time. His father was fighting for his life a few feet away and it would not help his recovery to listen to them quarrel.

By the door, he looked back again, but Rose's head was bent as she began arranging the clean sheets so it would be easier to change them.

Mr Watkins was coming up from downstairs, no doubt to help roll his father while Rose changed the sheets beneath the old man. Richard hated the flash of jealousy he felt when Rose gave a friendly smile to the valet and began chatting away, still the amiable young woman to everyone else but him.

'That always feels much harder than it should,' Rose said as she collapsed into the chair by the side of Lord Digby's bed.

Now they were changing the sheets daily. Doctor Griffiths had suggested keeping the environment as clean and aired as possible to give Lord Digby the greatest chance of recovery. The windows were always open, letting in the summer breeze, and they had limited the number of candles to be used in the room in the evening. The hardest part was the daily sheet change, with rolling Lord Digby from one side to the other while stripping out the old sheets from underneath him and tucking fresh ones in a physical challenge. Rose and Mr Watkins had got into a little routine now, but she still came out of it feeling hot and bothered.

'I will take these downstairs. Can I bring you some tea? Or even just a glass of water?'

'Water would be lovely, Mr Watkins, thank you.'

'Of course.'

Rose regarded the man in the bed. Earlier this morning she and Mr Watkins had washed and changed him into clean clothes, with Mr Watkins using his steady hand to shave his master. Now all she needed to do was a little light tidying and dusting around the room while she took her turn being with Lord Digby.

A flicker of movement caught her eye and she frowned, leaning in closer. Lord Digby had not moved for three days. His chest had continued to rise and fall, but his arms and legs had remained still and his eyes closed. She was convinced he was going to die and, although tragic, she wasn't convinced Lord Digby would have minded terribly. At least it was sudden rather than the protracted affair she had witnessed with her guardian.

The movement came again and Rose gripped the sheet. Lord Digby was tucked in up to his neck, and carefully she drew the sheet back just in time to see his hand moving a little. It was a jerky movement and at first she wasn't sure if it was involuntary, but after a minute he managed to reach up and scratch his chest. Then, as she watched, his eyes flickered open.

'Lord Digby, can you hear me?'

His eyes were unfocused, but now his lips were moving, although no sound was coming out. Rose leaned in closer, hoping she might be able to hear even a whisper.

'Water…' he said. 'Water.'

At that moment, Mr Watkins came back into the room with her glass of water.

'He's awake,' Rose said. 'Help me sit him up, he's thirsty.'

Lord Digby had been frail before his three days limited to the bed, but now he had hardly any fat on his bones. Between them, she and Mr Watkins were able to sit Lord Digby up, propping pillows behind him to ensure he did not fall to the side or slip down too much. Only once she was sure he was upright enough to swallow did she hold the glass of water to his lips.

He took a small sip and then another. Some of the water dribbled out of the corner of his mouth, but most went down.

'I can manage here. Go and tell Mr Digby and Lady Digby,' Rose instructed. The valet hurried out of the room.

By the footsteps that approached she could tell it was Richard who approached first, bursting into the room with a half hopeful, half disbelieving expression on his face.

'Father?'

Lord Digby did not reply, but he did look over at the sound of his son's voice, and Rose thought she saw a flicker of a smile on the old man's lips. Richard came and stood next to her, his hand resting on his father's.

'What happened?'

'We had just changed his sheets and I saw a small movement. I pulled back the sheet and it was his hand scratching his chest. Then he woke up.'

'I cannot believe it. I had given up hope.'

'I had, too,' Rose said.

She looked up at Richard, saw the relief in his eyes, the joy on his face, and for one moment she forgot how he had hurt her. For that moment she was just happy that his father had woken and he got to spend a little more time with the old man.

'Is it true?' Lady Digby said as she hurried in.

'Yes, my lady.'

'Henry, darling, you've had us so worried.'

Lord Digby looked bemused at the fuss, but continued to sip on the water that Rose held to his lips. Three days he had been without fluid and she did not doubt he was thirsty now.

'Shall we send for the doctor, my lady?' Rose said,

already motioning for Mr Watkins to go and find a groom to ride to Dr Griffith's house.

'Yes, please do. I cannot believe you are awake, Henry.' Lady Digby was looking at her husband in amazement, gripping his hand and kissing the top of his head. 'Perhaps we should give him a little space.'

Rose handed the glass to Lady Digby, stepping away from the bedside. She felt the tears falling on to her cheeks as she watched Lady Digby quietly sob as she held on to her husband.

'We will give you a moment, Mother,' Richard said, leaning down and dropping a kiss on to his mother's head.

They both retreated to the hall, closing the door quietly behind them.

'I cannot believe it.' Richard said, leaning back against the wall. He looked relieved and happy, but most of all stunned from the unexpected recovery.

'Me neither. I did not think—' She cut herself off before she could complete the sentence.

'I thought the same.'

'Especially after three days.'

'He has some strength left in him yet.' Richard ran a hand through his hair and shook his head with a disbelieving smile. 'Thank you for your help in his care.'

'It is my job,' Rose said, 'and, more than that, it was my pleasure to look after him. I care about both Lord and Lady Digby.'

'I know you do. It is one of the remarkable things about you. Even after your last employer treated you so badly you have space in your heart to feel affection for my parents.'

'I have met some cruel people in this world, but also some very kind ones. Your mother is one of the best.'

'I agree.'

Richard stood up from where he had been leaning against the wall and together they walked down the corridor towards the stairs.

'Rose…'

She turned to him and shook her head. 'Not now. I do not wish to spoil this moment. Whatever you have to say to me, can it wait until later?'

'A few more hours will not hurt. Will you meet me tonight?'

She sighed, but nodded. These past few days she had worked on blocking out the desire that flared within her whenever Richard was near. There was physical attraction, but more than that she wanted to be the person he turned to when he was uncertain, the one he discussed his problems with and the one he chose to celebrate his successes with.

It was hard to block these feelings out, but piece by piece she was building the wall around her heart to protect it. She wondered if tonight he would announce he was planning on leaving. That would be bad enough, but if he chose to stay at Meadow View, to build his life here, Rose was aware at some point she would have to move on. She would not be able to keep up the pretence of indifference when he moved on with his life.

'Perhaps in the folly at ten o'clock.'

'As you wish.'

Chapter Twenty-Four

Night had fallen about an hour earlier with a dramatic sunset in the west. The sky was heavy with clouds and the setting sun had lit them up as if they were plumes of ash being spewed from an active volcano. The air was close and heavy and somewhere in the distance Rose thought she might have heard the first rumble of thunder. She wanted it to rain, wanted the uncomfortable stickiness to lift and for the temperature to drop to a more reasonable level for May.

She had a grey dress on with a high collar, the one she had been wearing all day. It had been hard not to flop into bed once her duties for the day were done, but she knew it was important for her and Richard to talk one last time.

Despite everything that had happened, she still felt a fizz of excitement as she crept from the house and across the lawn. Quickly, she suppressed it. He had made it clear by his reaction after their intimacy that he did not want anything lasting to develop between them. She had been a welcome distraction when he was just realising he did not need to live his life in such self-imposed misery, but the only son of a baron did not marry a maid who had started life on the streets of London.

For her part, she cursed every time her heart skipped when he walked into the room. She didn't want to want him, but she had to acknowledge that sometimes hearts were irrational.

'You came.'

Richard's voice came out of the darkness of the folly, surprising her. She had been a few minutes early, unable to stand the terrible anticipation as she waited in her room for the hands on the clock to reach the agreed upon hour.

'Of course I came. We have important matters to discuss.'

'I was not sure you would. You have been avoiding me again.'

'You can hardly blame me.'

'No, you are right. I do not blame you.'

Rose was standing on the threshold of the folly and Richard just inside. It was a small building, built in the shape of a Roman temple and with a statue of Venus inside. It was empty except for one old bench, rescued from the garden when it had become too weather-beaten and half forgotten about in the depths of the folly.

As Rose contemplated whether she should enter a fat raindrop fell from the sky, landing on her head. It was followed by another and another, making her decision a little easier.

'Shall we sit?' Richard suggested.

They both sat tentatively on the rickety bench, testing it gingerly before sitting back.

'I am tired, Mr Digby—' Rose said, but Richard interrupted her.

'Richard, please call me Richard.'

She contemplated for a minute and then nodded. 'As you wish. I am tired, Richard. It has been a long few days and I wish to get to my bed. Say what you need to and then we can both retire.'

'You have been working hard.'

'It has been a trying few days for all of us.'

'I cannot believe we have only known one another a few short weeks, Rose.' He shook his head ruefully. 'So much has changed. *I* have changed so much and a lot of that is because of you.'

She remained silent, willing to hear what he had to say, but not able to summon the enthusiasm for discussion. Rose's heart was already broken, she did not wish to rub salt into the wound.

'When I arrived back in England, I was convinced I would stay only for a short while. I thought I needed to get back to my work in the Dutch East Indies, or wherever fate took me next, but I was exhausted and sick in my heart of all the moving, of never settling down, never having any fulfilling relationships.'

She nodded, remembering him when she had first seen him in St Ives. He had looked as though he was considering getting back on the coach to London before he had even set foot in Hemingford Grey.

'I was consumed by my guilt, wrapped up in these thoughts of needing to do some good in the world to try to make up for the bad decisions I had made. Then I met you.' He smiled at her warmly.

'I do not know how you did it. I wasn't even aware

of what you did, but you opened my eyes to the world outside my own troubles. You began to convince me that there was another way to live, to chip away at the guilt I carried until I began to wonder if you were right, if perhaps I could think of a normal life.'

'You make it sound more planned than it was. I merely wanted to show you that you did not have to live a life filled with guilt and self-recrimination all the time.'

'You did a good job.'

'Lady Cambridgeshire and Mrs Godrum helped.'

'They did. When I realised even they did not hold me responsible I realise how self-indulgent I was being, making the whole tragedy about me even all these years later. Frederick's death upended my world, but I was not the only one affected. Amelia had not forgotten her brother, but had managed to live a happy and full life, and Mrs Godrum in her own way allowed herself some enjoyment of her family while still mourning Frederick. I was the only one who had stopped his life because of the accident.'

It was the first time she had heard Richard refer to the tragedy as an accident. She tried not to react, tried not to make a fuss over his choice of words, but it made her feel happy, despite the fact she was here for him to end their relationship, whatever it had been.

He turned to her now and lowered his voice a little. 'I am not proud of how I acted after we left Mrs Godrum's house. I felt this sense of freedom, as if I had just been liberated from the darkest gaol cell, and all I wanted to do was experience the world and all its delights again after denying myself for so long.

'Ever since we first met I had been suppressing how I felt about you, but after I had spoken to Mrs Godrum it was as if I could finally start to admit what you meant to me, that I no longer needed to think my whole life needed to be about punishment. I was free to pursue something good and true.'

'I have told you I forgive you. I gave myself to you freely. I wanted it as much as you.'

'I kissed you, made love to you, despite you telling me what it was you really wanted. To find a nice man, to settle down and live a life free of scandal and emotional drama. I didn't offer you anything, I just took what I wanted.'

'I wanted it, too, in that moment.'

He closed his eyes and she saw he felt true regret.

'You told me how Mr Rampton made you feel, how he never considered your feelings, or if he did only so he could manipulate them. After, I felt I had done the same. I took what I wanted, without thinking about what it meant for you.'

She stayed silent. This was the crux of the matter. Once she had realised the idea of a future with Richard was absurd she had felt true heartbreak. It had only been then she had realised quite how much she had come to care for him.

'I am a cad, Rose. A selfish cad.'

'You are forgiven,' she said, shifting in her seat. 'Now may I return to the house?'

She saw the surprise in his face and realised he hadn't expected her to be so calm, so cold in her demeanour. She had done her crying in private and was determined not to cry here.

'Will you spare me just two more minutes?'

Outside, the rain continued to hammer down, bouncing a few inches off the ground each time a drop hit the stones. The thunder was getting closer now and Rose did not feel as though she wanted to run across the lawn while the storm was directly overhead.

'Two minutes, then I wish to get to bed.'

She pressed her lips together and looked down, hoping Richard wouldn't see how much it was costing her to be so aloof. If she was honest with herself, all she wanted was for him to turn back time and go back to the moment after they had made love. She wanted him to look down at her and declare his undying love before asking her to marry him.

It hadn't happened that way and it never would. Now too much had passed between them and it was too painful to even be close to him.

He turned to her, waited until she was looking at him. She was taken back to the times they had kissed and even now she felt the irresistible pull, drawing her in.

'I love you, Rose Carpenter,' he said, reaching out and taking her hand.

Rose almost fell off the bench, she was so stunned. Quickly, she scrambled to her feet, backing away from Richard as though she had just realised he was the devil.

'I love you with all my heart.'

'No,' she said, shaking her head. 'No, no, no, no, no.'

She seemed to be incapable of saying anything else.

'It is the truth. I love you. I love your beautiful smile and your kind heart. I love your patience and your desire to tell the truth even if at first it is a little painful. I love every little thing about you.'

She turned away, completely confused by his declaration. Richard stood and followed her, placing his hands gently on her arms and spinning her to face him.

'I love you and I want everyone to know.'

'You can't love me,' she managed to stutter.

'I do. I love you and I am going to tell the whole world.'

'Richard, no. We cannot be together, so, whatever it is you think you feel for me, you need to let go of this notion.'

'Love,' he said simply. 'What I feel for you is love.'

'No. If you loved me, you wouldn't have put me through what you have these last few days. You wouldn't have made love to me and then barely spoken a word to me since.'

'I am sorry, you are right—it was unacceptable behaviour, but it is not because I do not love you. I was still trying to work through everything in my mind. In a short space of time, I had realised my whole way of living, my whole way of thinking, was wrong. I needed to be sure of what my future could look like before I could drag you into it.'

He shook his head, speaking quickly now. 'I didn't want to declare my love for you and then realise my conscience and my guilt were driving me to leave England.'

'Why didn't you just tell me this? Why didn't you talk to me?' She shook her head, trying to work through the swirling emotions that were battling for prominence inside her.

'I should have, but it was taking all I had to convince myself that everyone around me was right and I needed to change how I lived.' He stepped closer and a thrum of attraction passed between them. 'I love you, Rose, and I want to be with you. Will you marry me?'

She stumbled back, shocked, shaking her head. It had been all she had dreamed of, but these last couple of days she had been made to face reality, to tell herself it could never have worked anyway.

'We cannot marry, Richard. I am a maid…you will be a baron one day.'

'What does it matter? I love you and I think you love me.'

'You know as well as I it would be impossible. We could not socialise with your peers; they would shun you for your poor decisions.'

'Then we go elsewhere. We can live anywhere, Rose, somewhere no one knows anything about us other than what we decide to tell them.'

'I do not wish to hide who I am.'

'I don't propose you should. All I am saying is that there is somewhere in this world that will accept us and our relationship. It may be closer to home than you think.' He paused, looking at her. 'Is that your only objection?'

'No.'

'Tell me, Rose,' he said, and she saw a flicker of panic in his eyes.

'After we made love, you treated me as your inferior. Not by ordering me about or tasking me with menial chores, but by ignoring me. If I were the daughter of some country gentleman, you would never have acted in that way, but you did because you knew I could do nothing about it.'

She saw the shock on his face as he realised it was

the truth. He had shut her out, kept her waiting, not involved her in decisions that affected her. It made her feel unimportant and she didn't want to feel like that for the rest of her life.

'Rose, I am so sorry. I didn't realise.'

She took a deep breath and tried to ignore the painful squeeze of her heart in her chest.

'I love you, Richard,' she said quietly. 'I truly wish we could live the life together that you imagine for us, but I don't think it would work. There would be part of you that will always remember where I am from, of the work I have done over the last few years, and I think it would mean we would not have a marriage that was a partnership. I can take orders and accept I am inferior when it is coming from the people I work for, but I do not want it in my marriage.'

With the tears flowing down her cheeks, she leaned in and kissed him on the lips, savouring what she knew would be their last kiss. Part of her was screaming silently, telling her she was making the worst mistake of her life, but still she managed to turn away and walk out of the folly into the pouring rain.

Richard felt as though his heart had been ripped out of his chest while it was still beating. For a moment he could only watch Rose walk away. He had been so intent on the things that had stopped him being able to commit to her that he had completely ignored how he had made her feel. No wonder she had refused him now.

'No,' he murmured, 'I can't lose her.'

The idea of life without her seemed bleak and empty. He didn't even want to contemplate it.

'Rose,' he shouted as he rushed out into the rain. 'Wait.'

For a moment, he thought she might ignore him, but she did stop, turning to face him. Already she was soaked. The rain was torrential and as he reached her a flash of lightning cracked overhead, illuminating the sky.

'Please, Rose. I love you. I was inconsiderate, but I can do better. Please do not throw what we have away.'

He saw the uncertainty in her eyes and realised then she did truly love him. It was hurting her as much as it was hurting him, her decision to walk away.

'We are not equal,' he said, reaching out for her hand. 'You are my superior in so many ways. Without you I would still be a guilt-ridden wreck, ready to run off and bury myself in a natural disaster in the hope I could ease my conscience a little. You are beautiful and kind and clever.' He held up his hand to stop her from interrupting. 'But I know that is not what you mean by equals and I agree. As a man I have an advantage anyway, but what if I made what I could equal between us?'

'You cannot change anything,' she said, but she didn't walk away.

'I can. When I inherit, I will get the lawyers to sign over half the money and half the property to you. You will have the same income I do, the same land, the same number of properties. Before that I will sign over half of my investments. I know money is not everything, but it will mean you are independent, not reliant on me for anything. If you chose to spend your money on a trip to Italy or fifty new dresses, then there will be nothing I can do to stop you.'

'I do not want your money, Richard.'

'I know, and it is not really about the money, it is about trying to equalise things.'

For a long while she was silent, her eyes searching his as they stood in the torrential rain. Thunder and lightning raged overhead, but he would wager Rose didn't even notice.

'You would do that for me? Make me your equal partner?'

'Yes, a thousand times yes. I would sign everything over to you if it meant I got to spend my life with you, but I think you would prefer equality.'

'I would.'

'Then what do you say? Be my wife, my partner. I vow to share every decision, every part of our lives, equally.'

She launched herself forward into his arms and kissed him, their lips wet from the rain. He didn't care about the downpour, all he cared about was that the woman in his arms was going to be his wife.

They staggered back to the folly, gasping as the rain subsided under the shelter of the roof. Rose was completely drenched, her hair stuck to her face and shoulders in thick ropes. Her dress was plastered to her body, and he could feel the weight of her skirt, heavy with water.

'I love you, Rose Carpenter,' he said as he kissed her.

She wrapped her arms around his neck and pressed her body to his. He felt the desire rise inside him and with a rush of ecstasy realised that soon they could spend all day, every day, in bed together and it would be no one's business but theirs.

With one hand, he closed the door to the folly, leaving them in almost complete darkness, and then with the other he ran his hands down Rose's back, only stopping as she let her head fall back and a soft moan escaped her lips.

'I love you, Richard,' she murmured into his neck.

Those words lit a fire inside him and he picked her up, resting her back gently against the wall and using his free hand to lift her skirts. In the darkness he could see her eyes gleaming, and he loved the way they widened as he touched her teasing with his fingers while she moved underneath him.

'Within a month we will be married,' he said as she let out another moan. 'Within a month you will be Mrs Rose Digby.'

She raised her head up and kissed him. 'Mrs Rose Digby,' she murmured. 'I like that.'

As she writhed in pleasure under his touch, he pushed inside her, banishing the fleeting thoughts of guilt that he should not be allowed to experience such happiness as this.

After, they spent a little time sat on the rickety bench. Richard had his arm wrapped around Rose and they sat mainly silent, just enjoying being together. Much later it was time to return to the house, to their separate bedrooms, but Richard pushed away any irritation at the thought by reminding himself that soon he would be married to the woman he loved.

Chapter Twenty-Five

'You look stunning, my dear,' Lady Digby said as she fussed around Rose, tweaking the skirt of her dress so it flowed out behind her.

It was four weeks since Rose had agreed to marry Richard, four weeks of blissful anticipation. Although they had no real need for a rushed wedding, Richard had applied for a Special Licence. He did not have the connections normally needed to smooth a request such as this, but together he and Rose had visited the Archbishop of Canterbury after Lord Cambridgeshire had been kind enough to organise the meeting. Richard had explained the sad situation with his father and asked for a special licence to be granted so they could be married at Meadow View.

Lord Digby had recovered somewhat from his head injury, but his mobility had reduced and with it his confidence. They had realised that if they had organised a church wedding it was unlikely Lord Digby would have been able to attend.

The Archbishop had been sympathetic to their cause

and later Rose had learned he had witnessed a simi-lar affliction as Lord Digby had in his own mother. The Special Licence was granted and it meant today the wedding was to take place in the drawing room at Meadow View.

'I think this might be the happiest day of my life,' Lady Digby said, squeezing Rose's hand.

'I know I am not the daughter-in-law you expected...' Rose said, and Lady Digby straightened, a stern look on her face.

'You are everything I could hope for in a daughter-in-law,' she said firmly and then sighed. 'I admit if you had told me ten years ago Richard would marry a maid then I might have been less thrilled, but I think that just shows that you never know what twists and turns life will take. What might have seemed like a disaster then you now realise is the biggest blessing of your life.'

She took Rose's hands in her own and beamed. 'Thank you for saving my son. I believe that without you he would be soon disappearing back to dangerous places to try to assuage his guilt.'

'Thank you for welcoming me into your home and your family,' Rose said, trying to blink away the tears in her eyes.

'Look at us, sobbing already,' Lady Digby said, step-ping away and fiddling with the bouquet of flowers she had picked herself from the meadows outside for Rose to carry with her. 'Now I had better make sure Henry is settled and comfortable. Good luck, my dear.'

When Lady Digby had gone, Rose took a moment to look at herself one last time in the mirror. To the little girl who had grown up on the streets of London, pushed from one uninterested relative to another, the woman standing here today would be unrecognisable.

Today Rose did not feel nervous. There were only a select few close friends and family attending the wedding ceremony, people who all knew about Rose's past in one way or another and were happy to see Rose and Richard marry.

With one final look around her, she picked up the wild flower bouquet and made her way downstairs. She paused for a moment outside the drawing room, catching a sight of Richard as he stood in front of the window, waiting for her. He looked happy, carefree even, although she knew he would never be rid of all his demons. Sometimes he still had nightmares, calling out in the night, but soon she would be there to soothe him as soon as they started.

She had no one to walk her into the room, to hand her over to Richard, so instead she raised her chin and walked in by herself. Soon, she would never be alone, she would always have the love and support and protection of her husband, and the thought made her even happier.

She walked past Lord and Lady Cambridgeshire on one side, grappling with their numerous children, all of whom fell silent as Rose walked in. On the other side of the room sat Lady Digby, holding her husband's hand, with Mr Watkins discreetly behind. The rest of the servants were huddled together at the back. Invited guests, but a little uncertain of their place here in the drawing room.

Rose noticed them all as she passed, but her eyes were locked firmly on Richard, never wavering until she reached his side.

'You are beautiful,' he murmured as he took her hand. 'Are you ready?'

'Yes.'

'Then let us begin our life as husband and wife... and as equals.'

Epilogue

'Come, Constance, we went over this yesterday,' Rose said, smiling at the young girl. She was waif-thin and missing her middle front teeth, so spoke with a lilting lisp.

Squinting at the slate blackboard, Constance read the letters of the alphabet. She did so slowly, but this time without any mistakes. The other children in the class listened carefully, aware they could be called upon next.

Before Rose could ask another child to demonstrate their learning, a bell rang from somewhere deep in the building and the children all sat up a little straighter. It was lunchtime, the favourite time of day of every single pupil at Meadow View School for the Destitute. Rose smiled at the class and dismissed them, watching as they rushed to get a good spot in the large lunch hall.

Her smile broadened as she caught sight of Richard striding down the wide corridor.

'Good afternoon, Lady Digby,' he said, bending down to kiss her. Three years after their marriage and his passion for her had not cooled. Every time they parted, she knew he would greet her with a kiss. 'How was your class today?'

'Wonderful. I love teaching.'

Rose did not normally spend her days teaching, but one of their regular teachers had been unwell with congestion in the lungs and Rose was only too happy to step in for a few weeks. It made a nice difference from the administrative side of things that was normally her responsibility.

After they had married, Rose and Richard had talked a lot about the work he had done in different countries around the world. Even though he was not proposing he return to that way of life he had been keen to do something charitable with his time. Rose had been the one to suggest they go back to her roots to find their cause. It had taken a lot of work, but a year earlier they had opened their school for the poor children of St Giles and the surrounding area. It was free and, what was more, they provided the children with a hot meal every single day. Rose knew it was sometimes the only food these children received.

The first day they had opened only three children had turned up, but over time word had spread and now they had a long waiting list. Much of the day-to-day running was done by the teachers they employed, paying well over a basic wage to attract intelligent women who cared about the children in their care. It meant Rose and Richard could now split their year between Meadow View in Hemingford Grey and the school in London.

'Mama,' Emily called, her voice loud enough to carry across half the school. On little legs, the two-year-old barrelled towards them, grinning as she threw her arms around Rose's legs.

'I am sorry, Rose, I couldn't stop her,' Lady Digby said as Rose bent down and picked her daughter up, covering her with kisses.

'I do not mind. Lessons have finished for the day. What have you been doing with your grandmother, Emily?'

'Boat on lake,' she said in her usual matter-of-fact way.

'That sounds wonderful. Perhaps you could take me and your father to the lake tomorrow and we can try sailing your toy boat.'

'Ices.'

'Yes, if you are a good girl, we will stop in the park for ices.'

'Come now, Emily,' Lady Digby said, taking the little girl back into her own arms. 'Your mama and papa will be home soon, but first we need to go and ask cook to start preparing the lunch.'

Rose watched fondly as Lady Digby walked away, holding Emily's hand, head bent down so she could hear everything the child could say.

'We should talk to the teachers and then we can be done for the week,' Richard said. He had a spring in his step as they walked down the corridor together and for a moment Rose marvelled at how different he was from the man she had first met three years ago at Meadow View. He was happy now, contented in his work and in the role of baron and landowner now he was Lord Digby. His father had passed away six months after Rose and Richard's wedding. It was not unexpected, with the old Lord Digby becoming increasingly frail until he was struck down and carried off by a winter fever. They had all mourned him and missed him, most especially Lady Digby, but with the birth of Emily a few months later it gave them something positive to focus on.

'I think it is the start of summer,' Richard said as he dropped a kiss on Rose's head. 'We should return to Hemingford Grey next week and to our favourite spot in the meadow.' He said it with a mischievous glint in his eye and Rose smiled at him.

'You have nefarious plans for me, I see.'

'Always, my love.'

Hand in hand, they walked into the small room they used as an office and where every Friday they were in London they met with the three teachers who ran the school and taught the classes. Richard took a seat in the corner, allowing her to take control of the meeting. He had been as good as his word three years earlier and even to this day he was meticulous in making sure they were equal partners in everything. Slowly they had found their strengths when it came to running a charitable organisation the size of the school and now, instead of splitting all tasks evenly, they were dividing things a little differently, taking on the jobs that suited their skills.

Once the meeting was finished, they checked on the lunch hall, pleased to see the children had finished eating and were heading home. One of the teachers took responsibility for locking up, so they followed the children out to the street.

As they approached the carriage that would take them home, Rose glanced over at the street corner where she would often sit, cold and hungry, begging for money or scraps of food when she was seven or eight years old. No one sat there now and the children that brushed past them had smiled on their faces and full bellies.

'Are you happy, Lady Digby?'

'Happier than you could ever know.'

* * * * *

If you enjoyed this story,
make sure to read
Laura Martin's
Matchmade Marriages miniseries

The Marquess Meets His Match
A Pretend Match for the Viscount
A Match to Fool Society

And check out some of her other recent stories

The Housekeeper's Forbidden Earl
Her Secret Past with the Viscount